A COLLECTION OF E DIFFERENT AUTHORS.

SUBJECTS:

Money debt slavery,
Destractive Economics,
World Governments.
Rule of World Corporations.
Modern Socialism.
Money and Wealth.
The contrast between Rich and Poor.

ALL PENETRATED WITH THE SPIRIT OF NEOSOCIAL JUSTICE.

Author and Collector:
Rudolf Rickes.

Web side:
http://www.rudolfrickes.com/

Trafford
PUBLISHING™

Order this book online at www.trafford.com
or email orders@trafford.com

Most Trafford titles are also available at major online book retailers.

Note for Librarians: A cataloguing record for this book is available from Library
and Archives Canada at www.collectionscanada.ca/amicus/index-e.html

Printed in Victoria, BC, Canada.

ISBN: 978-1-4251-7841-3 (soft)
ISBN: 978-1-4251-8107-9 (ebook)

*Our mission is to efficiently provide the world's finest, most comprehensive
book publishing service, enabling every author to experience success.
To find out how to publish your book, your way, and have it available
worldwide, visit us online at www.trafford.com/10510*

Trafford rev. 9/10/2009

Trafford
PUBLISHING™   www.trafford.com

North America & international
toll-free: 1 888 232 4444 (USA & Canada)
phone: 250 383 6864 ♦ fax: 812 355 4082

PAGE NUMBERS AND DESCRIPION OF ESSAY'S.

An Extract
From Joe Sobran.

History offers much to support this pessimistic view. Someone has estimated that mankind has been at war, on the average, for 13 years for every year of peace. And the wars have generally been wars of annihilation, no holds barred. "Civilized" warfare, sparing noncombatants, has been almost exclusively Europaen, existing chiefly in the eighteenth and nineteenth centuries, when war was sometimes almost gentleman's pastime, rather like foxhunting

So far, Joe Sobran

The above mentiones statements will not be rejected by me as utter nonsense. They contain a grain of bitter truth and must be recognized by all sane people. But, because of that, it should not lead to doomsday prognosis and shoulder shrugging, leaving things as they are. This is a human matter and therefore under human controll, and we can do something about it.

All noble and intelligent people, who not despair, should band together and attempt to impose changes of the root causes, as they see them. Most important the money slavery and other evils, as mentioned in my book "Social Justice, Yesterday, Today, Tomorrow". Creating a positive environment is already half the job done.

As a prominent example, is the exploitation and mistreatment of human as slaves, which was condoned by all nations and societies in the known world for thousands of years. Today, this has been proclaimeds immoral and considered finally illegal by 98% of the world.

Throughout history, individuals have stood ap aut of personal honour and sympathy for the slaves, depite the hoplessnes of their cause, to feight for the abolishment of slavery, just as I am fighting to overcome the evils of economic and debt slavery by the controlling Elite.

Improving the wrongs only to a degree, is already a success!

By the way, I believe to be in good company together with the Dalai Lama , Mahatma Gandhi and the late Dr. Martin Luther King,

The Author: Rudolf Rickes

Rudolf Rickes
AMICA at City Centre
 # 421380 Princess Royal Drive
Mississauga – Ontario
L5B – 4M9
Canada

ABOUT MYSELF.

I was born on August 3. 1920 in a small farming village close to a large city in the Rheinland of West Germany. Together with my brother, born a year earlier and my first sister, born four years after me, wer we three children. Our house stood on a slope and the road leading to the village, surrounded by forests, fields, meadows and a fruit garden.

My first impressions and years of life wer imprinted by nature around us. In outdoors, we only played in the forsts and meadows, pets were our welcome companions, or we stalked like hunters the then still plentiful wildlife.

My father was working as a craftsman in a company near the large city. With 6 years, I was inrolled in a public school, which I kompleted 8 years long with good report cards in 1934. After my discharge, I joint a company and became an apprentice for 4 years to learn Tool and Die making and received my diploma as a skilled craftsman.

In the fall of 1940 I was drafted into the German Airforce and got trained for 3 months on light antiairkraft guns and because of my technical skills, I was selected for an other 3 months training as a maintenance Soldier. After my discharg, I was send to occupaied Norway and joint an Antiairkraft Battery near the Airport "Sola" by Stavanger. I remeined there until all German Forces were internet by the British Army which became the new occupaier. The War was over and I was discharged in the Spring of 1945 as a Corporale.

At home, the civic damage was severe but I was not dis-spirited and found work in my profession with my former company.To improve my knowledge and climb-up the ladder of cuccess, I took every opportunity which came my way and enrolled onest for two years in eginering Studies on weekends and after that, one year every weekday – evenings classes in "production control" and "Time study", both with diplomas. As a resalt of this, I could change my job to better pay and worked as a design draftsman in an engineering department. In the fall of 1959 I proved my luck and emigrated to Canada with almost no knowledge in the english language. But I was lucky, I found a job as a machinist in a small Company, lernt in the evinings in special classes english and answered an ad in a news paper for an engineering technician. I got the job and stayed in this company untill my retirement in 1985. I was first desing draftsman and later the manager of the planning department.

During the years of my work, I experienced the "Social Problems" first hand around me which led me to the conclusion to write about it and when in 1998, I bought a computer and learnt it to use, I wrote first in German the book "Der Glaskäfig" and later "Soziale Gerechtigkeit etc", which a professional tranlater into english translatet. Eg."The Glass Cage" and "Neo Social Justice etc". The other books I compilet later from Newspaper cuttings and what I happened to read in books EG. "Common Dividend" and "Remarkables.

By the way, the German books "Der Glaskäfig" and "Soziale Gerechtigkeit etc" are both printed and published in Germany. Thank you for reading so far: Rudolf Rickes.

Why Is Socialism Still Important Today?

AN ESSAY BY: RODOLF RICKES.

The word "Socialism" and the associated concept have been vilified to such a degree, that merely writing about it and seeking an audience, has become en act of daring. Yet the Term was used in political literature for mor then a century, before being reduced to a disqualified buzzword. This is largely the foult of hothheads and criminal agitaters, who misused it in their lust for power over their own people. In this context one need only name Lenin in Russia (USSR) or Pol Pot in Cambodia. They abused the faith of their people's in a better future for the lower social strata, as well as their people's understanding of neosocialism as a deliverance from their misery.

Pleas note, that I am not advocating the "socialism" that was associated with class warfare for decades and which has been rightly condemned. I must emphasize that I only associate those ethical and noble characteristics with the term, that would also come to the mind of the man on the street, who is otherwise uneducated in such matters.

I would like the term "neosocialism", as I use it, understood as having arisen from the biblical principles of **loving your neighbour and doing good to those who hate you**. It is also my firm belief, that actions by neosocialists must not hinder other humans in any way or form, except to stop obvious and determined criminal behaviour.

RESPECT FOR HUMAN RIGHTS MUST BE THE SUPREME GUIDING PRINCIPLE.

Like others, neosocialists have had to learn from bitter experiances, yet thy remain convinced of the noble nature of their cause, despite all their setbacks.

The dogmatic neosocialism of class warfare, that was proclaimet by Marx and Engels a century ago – the proponents of which used force to establish it as a political systems-among their peoples – is now obsolete. It almost goes without saying, that democratic principles are a precondition to neosocialists thoughts, and that democracy and neosocialism complement one another.

Nowadays, whenever someone publicly exposes injustices, accuses them to the poor social behaviour of the perpetrators and tries to rectify the situation, he or she is promtly branded as a "socialist" and thus stigmatized and silenced.

As a school of thought, democracy developed gradually over the cours of centuries in various countries – admittedly not without violenc at times – and the spirit of neosocialism must also develop gradually and organically in the same way. It is not possible to legislate morality and so it would be equally wrong to attempt to spread democracy or neosocialism by force. Offering assistance is acceptable, but only without coercion, and only when one's own house is in order.

As previously mentioned, achieving the goal of a democratic, socially—oriented community of nations, depends entirely on an outwart – looking education whitout bigotry. In that respect, it is important to step in early to prevent articulate, Power—hungry characters from shrewdly pursuing their respective agendas, and it requires maximum vigilance on the part of all democrats and neosocialists to nip such developments in the bud.

I must however highlight the monopoly of the banks and their control over money markets which is destroying national Economies. If this monopoly is not broken by democratic and socialst leaders – an action that must be borne by the will of the people — all attempt to improve the living conditions of the people are in danger of failure. I therefore warmly recommend to read the book from the author "Common Dividend".

Taking Back Control Of Our Money Supply

BY JOSEPH W. DUGGAN
Shared Vision Magazin – June 1998

Money is the lifeblood of a technological society and it is extremely easy for a mere handful of individuals to control billions of people, if they own and control the banking system. Most of us have heard of the golden rule, whereby whoever owns the gold, makes the rules. What we have forgotten is, that we own the gold and letting an elite banking group make the rules, which serve theit narrow self—interest at the expense of the vast majority of humanity.

What is Money?

Initialy, money had intrinsic value in gold and silver coins, the weight of which represented a certain value in goods and services. Later on, notes were printed which were redeemable in gold and silver and, although once removed from precious metals, had intrinsic value as well. Currently, money is purely an agreed-upon medium of exchange for goods and sercices based on faith in the ability of the issuing country, to make good its financial obligations. Under this system, money has no intrinsic value, but whoever creates and controls it, can charge for the use of it. This is how the principle of charging fees for the use of money came about.

During the thousand-year, biblicaly-inspired ban on usury in the Middle Ages, lending Institutions could only charge fees (not interest), and engage in investment of their clients money. This resulted in an unparalleled time of prosperity, when massive cathedrals and the entire infrastructure of Europe were built. The sole purpose of interest is to enrich the few holders of capital at the expense of everyone else. The true producers of wealth— the artisans, tradespeople, inventers, workers, businesses people, etc – are slaves to the money masters who, whit their compound interest system, create more debt than there is money in circulation to pay for. Through propaganda, we are told that the few scraps from their banquet tables served to us as interest on our savings and RRSPs, justify their whole system. Nothing could be further from the truth.

WHERE DOES MONEY COME FROM?

The average person thinks that the government prints the money supply and that banks lend the money we have deposited with them as savings. These are to be the two biggest lies ever forced upon us. In Canada, the government currently creates $1 - 2\%$ of our money supply. We have in circulation abut 7% of our money suppley as paper notes printed by the Bank of Canada – not the federal governmet. The rest of our money sup-ply has been created by the private banking institution as a debt or loan.

Banks create money by making book entries, or computer entries, based on the collateral of the borrower. Basically, the real wealth of the borrwer, - his house, land, car, labour, etc – is pledged against the value of the loan requested. The lending institution merely creates a book entry aut of thin air and presto, the borrower has a deposit in his bank account or a cheque in his hands. For this book entrey, the bank collects interest at a rate as low as 4% (in the 1960s) to as high as 28% (in the early 80s). At one time, Canadian banks were required to maintain cash $5 - 7\%$ reserves, limiting them to creating 26 times their reserves in loans.

Currently, they have no limitations on the amount of money thy can literally create out of thin air. This is a lot of control in the hands of individuals, notorious for greed, corruption, and disregard for the interests of people, society and the environment.

We now live in the age of usury, wherebay some 99% of the increase in our money supply every year, is created as debt by lending institutions and requires that interest be paid on it. However, only the loan is created by lenders, not the money to pay the interest. The money needed to pay the interest doesn't exist. The interest can only be paid out of the 1 – 2% of the money supply created by the government. This is the basis of usury charging compound interest which creates more debt than can be paid by the money in circulation. Therefore, the charging of interest on loans results in debt, forecloser and seizure of assets pledged to "secure" the loans.

When loans are written by lending institutions, figures are entered into a computer, the credit is then deposited into the borrower's account and the money supply has increased by that amount. Excessive increases in the money supply as loans leads to inflation and spurts of economic growth. When loans are paid off and interest rates rise, recessions, depressions, foreclosers and bankruptcies occure.These "business cycles" are very painful and extremely damaging for the economy and ways to correct the underlying flaws of the fractioal reserve system.

A major, fatal flaw in our money system is, that whenever a loan is paid off, a corresponding portion of the money supply is destroyed. This is why our national or personal debts can never be paid off. It would eliminate our money supply. The great depression happened because the mony supply was so diminished by tight money policies of the banks, that there was not enough money in circulation for people to buy and sell goods and services. This is tremendous power to have concentrated among an elite group which meets secretly behind closed doors. The interest system can be eliminated when fees for the use of money, taken out of the principal borrowed loan and their would also no compounding interest anymore. No wonder that the term "usury" is so seldom used now-adays by economists; it actually describes how our economy works, and that's the last thing the money masters want us to know.

OUR GOVERNMENT IS CONTROLLED BY THE MONEY ELITE.

It stands to reason, that whoever controls the money, the government spends, controls the government policies and politicians. In Canada, the federal government owns all the shares of the Bank of Canada (BOC), but has no voting power, even though the Minister of Finance has a seat on the Board of Directors. This is supposedly to separate the banking system from the excesses of uncontrolled government spending. However, the BOC is directly under the control of the bank of International Settlements in Geneva, Switzer-land, which dictates to all the member banks.

SOFAR JOSEPH W. DUGGAN
THE BIGGEST THIEF OF ALL IS STILL AT LARGE!

BY LOUIS EVEN!

There are as many different sorts of thieves as there are kinds of thievery. There are highwayman, holdup artist, pirates, rustiers and hijackers, shoplifters, pickpokets, housbreakers, purse snatchers, and those who practice embezzlement, blackmail, fraud, swindling and extortion. And that by no means exhaust the list.

Now, there is one particular thief whom we have been denouncing for a long time. But he is still at large and the Law is making no attempt to lay hands on him; in fact he is held in high respect by the authorities. This particular robber excells in the art of swindel and extortion.

Our regular readers have propably guessed who it is; yes it's the old thief, the existing financial system, whos agents operate boldly among us in the broad light of the day. The fact that its technique is considerred to be a secret mystery by layman, plus the fact that its activities have been sancioned by the law, permits it to carry out its depreciations on an unheard-of scale without its victims ever guessing, who it is that is depriving them of th overflowing bounty which natur and man's ingenuity has to offer. Oh, they know very well that they are being robbed right and left, but this crafty old thief is skilled in turning his victims one against the other, making each believe that the other is responsible for his losses.

A SWINDLE.

Even those who are fairly well informed know that over nine-tenths ot the money that is up into circulation is born in the banker's ledger, taking it's form and substance from the banker's pen and a few drops of ink; and the other one-tenth, the paper money and coins, can only come into existens through an order. No one can deny, with reason, that all this money, ones brought into existence, is considered by the banke as their property which they can lend aut at a profit to themselves. But how many people have ever stopped to consider the scope and extend of this vast swindle? For there is no gainsaying that this contract entered into between the lender of this new money and the individual or corporation who mey borrow it is nothing less than a barefaced swindle.

The man who wishes to borrow money to build a factory, has to give the banker collateral or security for the loan; this collateral is real wealth, his own goods. A municipality borrowing money has to give, as its sesecurity, the right to tax the citizens, its power to mortgage the property of those under its jurisdiction. And what has the banker to offer? Well, he wants us to believe that he is lending the bank's money. In fact, all he is giving is a number of figures issuing forth from his pen and ink, but the value of these figures is not based on the banker's pen and ink, but on the work and products which came from the borrwer himself.

Note, to explain the riddle about what kind of money we are talking here. First, there is the money in circulation – coins and paper bank notes in various denominations obtainable by everyone – and second, numerals on various ledgers at businesses or governments as a result of a borrowing Agreement with the bank.

The one borrowing, brings the fruit of his labour – real concrete wealth, goods which can be used by all. The lender brings nothing more then a few figures scribbled in a ledger. And what happens? The one, who has no real wealth to offer, sees to it, that he is reimbursed, not only with the amount of money represented by his figures in a ledger, but with an other amount, over and above the new money issued, which is called **Interest,** which the poor borrower has to get from the money that is already in circulation, thus making it impossible for someone else to meet his finacial obligations. For, the lender did not put into circulation the amount necessary to cover the interst charges.

So it happens that the people, as a whole, are put into debt for the wealth which they, as a whole, have produced. This is where the swindle occurs. To have to pay for the goods one has produced, and more then their value, would be something unthinkable among individuals. If you build a table for yourself worth twentyfive dollars, it would be considered absolutley ridiculous to everyone that you should hav to pay some department of the government or some private individual for having build yourslf this table. Yet such rediculous thing is happening wher the people of a country, as a whole, are considered in relation to those individuals who are concerned with making modern money.

Those who have obtained the exclusive right of manufacturing money, oblige those who have no right to create even a cent of new money then what has actually been put into circulation. Such a system can have only one end – the plunging into debt of the entire world, right to the end of time. Unless, of course, it is decided to put an end to this universal swindle.

EXTORTION.

But the robbery doesn't end there. This swindle is compounded with extortion. What do we mean by "extortion"?

Extortion has been defined as the offence of obtaining, by threat or force, money or valuables not due. Gangs of organized criminals will obtain from businessmen periodic payments of money, under the threat of wreaking damage upon their businesses. This is a story everyone is familiar with, from movies and from crime reports in our daily newspapers.

Well, believe it or not, our existing financial system is practicing just such a crime. even though it has been legalized by our governments. Production today cannot be organized unless there is first of all money whit which to pay for operations before the first products can

be sold. **Any expansion of the productive system requires an expansion of credit by the financial system. The financial system imposes its condition, and if you do not agree to these conditions, you simply do not produce or expand. The financial system paralyzes you by withholding the credit.**

The financial system commits extortion by actally saying; Either you sign this document committing yourself to bringing me such and such an amount periodocally, or else, I will tie your hands by refusing you money, without which you can do nothing.

The budget of every public body has one sacred item, which is called "debt servic" the interest and capital which must be paid to the Financiers. Any other expense can be cut down and and pared off, but this particular item must never be touched. For this is a tribute which must be paid to the masters who are over the representatives of the people, just as they are over the people themselves. It is the ransom which must be paid for the right to live.

AN INSATIABLE RODENT.

In the issue of the book "Common Dividend" is written about that ubiquitious and voracious rodent which is present everywhere – the finacial system. This scourge is everywhere. It afflicts private as well as public corporations; it hits at the individual as well as the body politic. It is the prime cause of the high cost of living.

The system of finance is a devouring rat, a thief, a swindler, an extortionist – it is all these things and it leaves a trail of victims suffering from want and privation and insecurity. It humbles proud nations and brings people's government before it on bended knees. It will not hesitate to foment nations, destroying wars in orde to keep the world subject to it and paying tribute to it.

And yet nothing is done to halt the depredation of this great thief. It has as its protector the very elected representatives of the people. It has at its defenders those very men who should enlighten the way, castigate injustice and defend the opressed.

WORLD GOVERNMENT —UTOPIA OR REALITY? AIM OF THE FINANCIERS?

BY RUDOLF RICKES

Overview of subject-matter for a "world government"

This overview is an attempt to briefly describe for the interested reader the world government desired by so many, with the option of implementing it or rejecting it as an utopia. In common with many others, the author of these pages believes that Western Culture is declining and that this is therefore, a good time to radically change the old system states. Not that all my readers will agree with me, but I have hat at laest dared an attempt.

INTRODUCTION.

To those hwo had had the oportunity to red the book "The Ouline of History" by H.G. Wells, will be amazed how early and how often the rulsers and soverereigns of large kingdoms and empires strove to realize the idea of a single world government for all the people (in the respectively known world).

And it were not the rulers, but also the religions, who strove for this in order to increase the numbers of their followers and to spread their blessings to as much members as possible. Mentioned are Christianity, Judaism, Mohamedanism and etc. The extent to which other great religions such as Buddhism and Hinduism in Asia or religions in China attempted the same, is unknown to the authore.

However, in spite of all these endeavors, it was not the aim of the respective rulers and advocates of a "World Government" for all countries, to free the invidual citizems from their misery and offer them an easier, more beneficial and peaceful axistens, but rather only to aquire mor power and wealth without any competition.

This desire weaves its way through human history like a red thread, sometimes as a heazy dream , sometimes as a pampered beautiful illusion of those, with power over their people during the centuries before Christ and after, right up to the present day. It is well known, that even the polotical thinking of "Communism, with its slogan: "Worker of the World, Unite", desired and trough a revolution intended to enforce the power of the proletariat so thy, too, could enjouy the anticipated wealth.

The two world wars have given frish impetus of the idea and the hope of freedom from such conflicts between the nations of the world. Therefore, in 1919, the "Leage of Nations" was created, based on the 14 points of the American President Wilson, which led to an armistic to end the terrible fighting and to the hypocretical aim of guaranteeing peace forever. However, it became an assembly of querrals trough the fault of the victor nations and was rather weak and useless. After World War II, the victorious nations established in 1946 "The United Nations" with same propaganda aims as in 1919. To protect the world from new convulsions caused by wars and unrest and to contribute to understanding amongst nations, for the benefit of the whole world. Negotiations and communications instead of violece was and is still the motto of the so called "United Nations" in spite of wars in Korea, Virtnam, Balkan, Afghanistan and in Iraq, not to mention a few angagements in the past.

Then there is the "Bilderberg Club", a secret society of the wealthiest and most influential people in most of the contries of the western world, devoted to achieving a "World Government". The majority of the media is owned by this world elite and her and there, in newspapers or on television, it showers the population with its intentions, without mentioning the Bilderbergers's meetings and there existence.

Som articles on this subject even go so far as to demand, that any form of state power must be rejected (to make people happy). The say that no one may be forced and no one be subjected to any form of regulations made by another person without his ore her consent, unless he/she is a slave. However, such a completey free society of that sort, would be short lived, because envious neighboring states or criminal elements within the state would destroy and anslave it.

Before addressing in more detail the plan to create a "World Government", we must look at what form this desired world government should take and who should exercise power? That it must be a form of democracy goes without saying. Whether it includes the entire Globe or only the highly developed Western countries, will be a matter, for an intensive debate.

An endorsment of the idea of a society without the institutions of a normal state, which satisfies the before mentioned principles of independence and freedom of each individual citizen, must be rejected, because that would lead to "Anarchy".

Text books generally differentiate between three institutions of governmental powers or authorities, the legislative, executive and judicial powers. However, over the centuries, a fourth power has developed, namely the "Financial Power". This power, which governs all other powers and poceesses no authority from a constitution and is not subjectet to any government i.e. is not elected by the people, is the dreaded "Financial Power.

It is not the money that eveyone has in his wallet. It is not the money invested in shares and bonds or in bank savings accounts. Nor is the Financial power what governments call inflation, - the continuos increase in prices. No, those are all small fry compared with the status and the power of the superpower being denounced here and which believes, that it is the only power capable of governing the masses – with or without democrasy.

This "Financial Powere" is therefore reprehensible because it exercising authority with its decision to loan money which it does not have but which it creates out of nothing as a figure in its books, in return for "IN-

TEREST", the amount and term of which it determines, for everyone who needs money like Governments – central or provincial,- communities, towns, businesses, corporations and for every private citizen who ever needs money, like a mortgage for instance and so on. Whit this, it regulats the life blood of the entire national economy of every nation.

So, who in the "Fiancial Power" actually makes the decisions?

In addition to the Bilderberger Club, already mentioned, it is kontrolled by the "IMF" (Internationaler Monetary Fund), the world bank in "Bern" Switzerland, the U.N. and alle European central banks. Every well known Europaen member of government hat a time or another attended a Bilderberger Conference and even the Seccretary General of the NATO is a Bilderberger, This shows that the Club is intensively involved in politics.

There is another important but not well known group of powerful and influential people called "The Commission of 3000" who are also striving for world supremacy. Then there are the internationale or globale corporations, who all crave for global market dominations. It has already been mentioned, that the world power aspired, must have a true democratis form of government, supported by the citizens of nations, so as to guarantee a free and peaceful live for all.

My book "Neo Social Justice, Yesterday, Today, Tomorrow" discusses in great detail the principles of a Democracy and its originate in Greece around 450 B.C. under the rule of the Statesman "Pericles". Please note, the democratic form of a society is one of many, but it is the one that stood the test of time througout history and must be the preferred form. However, not a "Money Bag Democracy" as practiced in the U.S.A. One has to be Millionair in order to have any chance in an election.

Above all, and this is not merely a suggestion but rather a condition, to establish a "World Government", the ideas and principles of democracy must be understood, respected, desired and demanded from the grass roots of the ordinary citizens on. As with every thing which has to do with the four state powers and their agencies, without which there can be no government, it must be initiated and chosen not from above by the existing powers, but from below by the ordinary citizens.

If it is not possible in that form, then the attempt to create a "World Government" for all people must be deemed to have failed. Anything else or merely similar, is not accepable. In a "World Government", established on the above principles, "Neo Social Justice" must prevail and all laws and decisions made by the Authorities and their Agencies have to reflect that aspect.

Any other form of a "World Government", as the Financiers and the todays Power Elite have in mind, must be prevented by all means.

And it is also very important in order to achieve this, that all medias – Newspapers, Television and radios educate the masses with the slogan "Neo Social Justice" and the notion:

He who has freedom and rights, has above all "Obligations"

However, the guaranteed freedoms of each individual in this "World Government" must not serve to encourage "Anarchy", where everyone may do as he pleases. In fact, the question of how the "World Government" should be composed, has not yet been addressed. It must be a voluntary union of states, based on the will of the democratic minded peoples, similar to the "European Union", the differnce being, that all the member states give up their sovereignty but not their curency, which remains under the authority of its respective government.

All the member states in the "World Government" retain their three branches of powers as already explained, and add the four power – the "Financial Power", which must be now included, being responsible for controlling of the flow of money, the life blood of the economy. It meets the demand of capital in the state, like government, provinces, municipalities, the economy in general and privat individuals for mortgages.etc. by granting "Interestfree" loans through the banks for a one-time fee.

The benefits for all the citizen of such a "World Government" are:

1) Prevention of wars within the world order and no need for nationals armed forces.

2) The unavoidable merging of economics and markets, causes free flow of goods (products) and therefore lowe prices.

3) The necessity of a unify healthsystem and drug plan as well as pharmaceuticals for all citizens.

4) The urgent necessity for standardisation of labour regulations in all companies in the world order, including working hours, length of vacation, vacationpay, health care, retirement age, etc.

This eliminates the greates obstacle, preventing us from fully utilizing the capacity of the Population, namely interest on debt, which was imposed by the capitalistic Qulice and at the same time contributes to brideging the gab between rich amd poor. The word "Profit" must be anathema in the "World Government" because it is not capital that is the purpose of Yield, but rather welfare of the individual citizen.

It is unlikely that switching from today's economic order, with the accumulating of debt amounting to trillions of dollars in some places, to a "World Government" as described before, would go off without serious social and political strife. Those powers in Finance, Banks, Economics and International Corporations, who today rule as they see fit and would like nothing better then to rule the world, will fight with all their intrigue and might. To keep their "Sinecure", they will not shy away from spreding the most malicious lies and shedding crocodile tears about to, what they believe, is the unjust treatment thy are forced to suffer. It is to be hoped, that not a "third world war" is necessarily to rekindle the idea of a "World Government" as discussed here.

All those, who are positive understanding and in favor of this proposal for a "World Government" must be in words and deets support the loudable aim within the spirit of "neo neo social justice".

It is well known, that the idea and principles of democracy grew in people's mind for centuries, before achiving it's prensent recognition. In the same way, the idea of "neo social justice" must be spread to the peoples of the world, by any means of propaganda and influence because, as was already mentioned, the will and desire towards a "World

Government" must com from the grass rootes, from the masses and not from the upper classes und rulers today.

After a "World Government" has been established, the individual citizen must be educated from the cradle on about "Neo Social Justice". They must learn compassion and mercy, contribution and cooperation and not adhere to the capitalistic rule "The Winner Takes All". At the same time it can be assumed, that the money system has been successfully changed, according to the rules of "Commom Dividend" and the pursuit of the "Dollar", as it was a stable and menacing lifestyle in the old system, has been replaced.

Of course, the member states and the "World Government" itself, must have laws and regulationes for the benefit of all and which must be observed. Since the people in a "World Government", are either smart, cranks, energetic, malicous and energetic or spiritual not ab to date, this ar all human beings, afflicted with virtues and and vices, which makees also a police force a necessity for each member State and the "World Government" as well. It is not and must not become a playground for eccentric and asociale elemente.

Some points that are undesirable in the social structure of the "World Government" and must be observed and implemented:

1   Posession of weapons of any kind, whit the exeption of those employed in poblic safty, forst rangers and hunters, is undesirable.

2   Lotteries and casinos are undesirable.

3   Public health care for every citicen is obvious.

4   The Media, like radio, television, news papers and the like, in short all publications must be given strict orders to pablicize and prais "Virtues" and condemn "Vices"

5   Wether larg or small, states in the "World Government" are equel with respect to neo social justice. Larger states with an accordingly strong and more influental economy, do not have the right to dominate other smaller states

6   The sociale achievements of today;s modern or advanced nations, like "freedom of speech and religion" to assemble or the freedom to form professional associations such as labour unions etc. are accepted.

7   Private property of any kind is respected in the "World Government".

8   A larger Union of states like the "World Government" is also able to intervene earlier and more successful with help after natural disasters such as earthquackes, tidel waves, hurricanes, volcanic eruptions, droughts etc. or man made turmoils and terrorist acts.

In oreder to create the agencies of power in the "World Government", parties must be created whose politican's, after a democratic election, determine the type and direction of policies based on the will of the people.

All the positive forces in the "World Government" are called to exercise the greatest vigilance in order to prevent destructive forces from unfolding and causing harm and unrest in the population, like oratorical agitators, those obsessed with obtaining power and canning elements. The "World Government" must be protected from destruction within.

When God gave Mannkind "Freedom"
then with the obligation of greatest vigilance,
especely against people whit Power in sthe states.

Starting with the age of 20, all citizen of the "World Government" are taken part in a "Point System", executed by the states. For each subsequent year, it awards a point, if no misdemeanour's were reported from each person that are not in line with "Neo Social Justice". The greatest number of accumulated points permits the induvidual to enjoy social adventages such as a higher pension payments or other rewards as the case might be.

GOOD CONDUCT MUST BE REWARDED'

Natural, the centrel government, apart from the states governments of the "Worldgovernment" must receive extra power from the electorate, the people, so that orders from it have teeth and are obeyed to the letter of the law against the culprit. A repeat of the wicked experience with the "League of Nation" after World War I and the wretshed show of the "United Nations after World War II, has to be avoided at all cost.

That is my contribution to the subject and I cherish the hope, that this essey was not written in vain and that utopia will becom reality against all odds, sooner or later. To abolish the slavery took several centuries until it was achived, lets hope it will this time not take that long.

In conclusion I will tranlate a German Poem by LUDWIG UHLAND:

Freedom that I believe in,
that fills my heart.
Come with your light,
sweet angelig vision,
has no wish to com to the troubled world,
merely dancing only in the heavenly firmament.

A CRITICAL
REFLECTION

BY RUDOLF RICKES
Foreword

I have long considered the idea of recording my observations and critical conclusions concerning the jumble of information with which we are bombarded by the press, radio and television on a daily basis, as long as I still have time to do it.

The purpose of this continuous rain of more or less impotant news to which we are sub-jected, whether we want it or not is clear to me, as of course it is to the majority of all reasonably intelligent human beings. It is not simply the noble impuls of the bosses and those pulling the strings, to keep us abreast of the latest events, but rather to influence our opinion and shape it to their purposes. It is the same urge that well-known dictators of all persuasions used and still use today to perfection, to bend their dear subjects to their will.

NEWS MEDIA CONTROLLED

John Swinton, former Chief of Staff for the New York Times – 1953 toasting the inadequacy of his profession before the New York Press Club:

"...if I allowed my honest opinion to appear in one issue of my paper, before twentyfour hours my occupation would be gone.

The business of journalists is to destroy the truth; to lie outright; to pervert; to vilify; to fawn at the feet of mammon, and to sell his country and his race for his daily bread."

"You know it and I know it, and what folly is this toasting of an independent press? We are the tools and vassals of rich men behind the scenes. We are jumping jacks, and they pull the strings and we dance. Our talents, our possibilites and our lives are all the property of other men. We are intellectual prostitutes."

The following quotation of David Rockefeller, then Chairman of Chase Manhattan bank, speaking at the June 1991 Bilderberg meeting in Baden-Baden, Germany, is illustrative of this media control:

"We are grateful to the Washington Post, the New York Times, Times Magazine and other great publications whose directors have attended our meetings and respected their promises of discretion for almost forty years." He went on to ex-plain: "It would have be impossible for us to develop our plan for the world if we had been subjected to the light of publicity during those years. But, the world is more sophisticated and prepared to march towards a world government. The supernational sovereignty of an intellected elite and world bankers is surely preferable to the national autodetermination practiced in the past centuries"

Those statements speak for themselves and require no interpretation or explanation. I do not believe they reveal anything new, but the outspokenness is remarkable. We now know how we are directed and managed, and throughout the millennia it has always been so in the development of mankind and has been the cause of all the wars and revolutions we were obliged to go trough. Virtue and vice have always fought for predominance and always will. The circumstances and tools change, but otherwise everything remains the same – from birth, human nature is predestined to do so.

That is a fundamental truth which was already debeted by Chinese wise men and ancient philosophers thousands of years B.C. Whoever is able to reach for the book by Lao Tse, one of the earliest Chinese thinkers and philosophers, born around 604 B.C, will be touched by the spirit of the man. Namely by the timeless spirit that once developed in him. It is not a matter of understanding all the hidden nuances and trains of tought, but simply of getting a feeling for that strange spiritual urge to seek the ultimate thruth.

Even then, in the battle for political power they differenciated between the divine, good, lucid amd warm "YANG" and the earthly, dark, cold and evil "YIN". the believe that Yin and Yang are active in every human being.

But let us return to virtues, and vices, i,e, yin and yang. The libraries of the world are bursting with books on this subject if, as is mustv be, we include religious literature. So it would be superfluous to write about it again. Whoever, it must be nentioned that from time immemorial, religion has played an important role in people's lives. Their purpose was to explain the incomprehensibility of the world in which they lived and show the right goal in life- as seen by their founders, of course.

Among the mass of existing organic lifeforms in this world, the first humans were social creatures, like many others, and like them were subjectet to the survival instinct.

It is not the purpose of this essay to expand on the subject. My book "Social Justice etc. addresses all that in detail, and I warmly recommend reading it. My aim is to show that from the time, necessary ordes of living were established among the first groups, the strongest, the brightest and, above all, the most willy held the leadership and undestood how to use fraud and falsehood to retain that role for himself and his decendants or for a likeminded clique. With their absolute power, they were called kings. In other countries the had other names. Contrary to the people thy ruled over, thy held all the authority over life and death, peace or war.

That would change, however. In ancient time Greece, as it is known today, was a collection of small citystates with various independent social orders. Each had his own army. Those citystates, which were in their peak around 450 B.C., had a political order with a constitution as their form of power and which set out the political direction. This was essentially put into practice according to the earlier methods used by the tribes,whereby each member was allowewd his individual vote. The Greece called this "democracy", which originates from the word "demos" (people) and "kratos" (rule), i.e. rule by the people. Roughly speaking, this placed limits on the arbitrariness of rulers.

Regrettable, the Greece democracies were not to last very long. The envy and resentment of their barbarian neighbours were able to conquer them and restore the old system. A period of two thousand years passed between the fall of the democratic citystates in Greece and the establishment of today's constitutional denocratic forms of gevernmnent. Even in a wellfunctioning democracy of today, it would be a mistake to deny that it is possible for crafty agitators to misuse a position of power to the detriment of the people. In order to prevent this from happening, all members of the populace would be well advised to be extremely vigilant.

However, there is a huge difference between the noble and and progressive theory of a democracy as they are taught in schools and which the popolace believes and "Reality". Even the proposition in the American constitution – that power is exercised by the people for the people – are merely empty words. Nothing is further from this principle than the democracy currently exercised in the USA. Whoever believes that the individuals who, from time immemorial, have ruled and exploited the people through their craftiness and eloquence, have now struck ther colours and are content and satisfied with their fate , are under a dangerous illusion.

They have already succeeded in undermining the general understood and generally believed principles of true democracy and exploited them for heir powerhungry purpose.

As in ancient times it is evident, that the small non-producing class in power, leads a lucrative life at the expense of the producing masses. But that is not all. In order to utilize the will of the people for their own purposes, the press, television and radio are being manipulated as described previously. All the decisive positions in the formation of public opinion are occupied by these people and no one dares to show any opposition. In addition to that, in most cases they are multi-millionaires; and who, amongst the simple voters or groups of voters, has the wherewithal to fight for e new or better concept before parliament? In election campaigns there is shameless lying, deceit and fear mon-gering – whatever the power clique deems most suitable to achieve its goal, namely to maintain absolute power over the people.

CAPITALISM VERSUS NEOSOCIALISM

Capitalism is an economic order in which production is determined by interest in moneytary gain and in which people who own capital assets, determine the type, direction and extent of production. Neosocialism is a concept in which the individual human being and the society, in there he lives, is the measure of all things. His wellbeing is the pinnacle of all concerns. Unfortunately, social muddleheads and radical neosocialists used writings about Marxism und Communism, which terrified the entire western world, when, after the First Welt War, Lenin led a bloody and successful revolution in Russia, and founded the Union of Socialist States of Russia, the USSR, brought the idas of neosocialism in disrepute.

The fall of communism in the USSR led to the decline of communist parties in the western democracies and throughout the world. Besides liberal and conservative parties only neosocialism and capitalism re-mained as adversaries in the battle for power and the economic order in the nations. At the same time, it is historicaly a tragedy that neoso-cialism and capitalism are adversaries. Both, capitalism as a motor and neosocialism as a break, would be an ideal vehicle with the aim of an economic sound society.

WHY "NEOSOCIALISM" TODAY?

Today the word "Socialism" and the associated concepts are so reviled that it is risky to write about it and to interest the reading public in it. But for over a century it was used in politicacal literature before being reduced to a degrading catchword and looked down upon. This not least because, as already mentioned, muddleheads and criminal agitators uti-lized it out of hunger for power over their peoples. Mind you, I am not in favour of the "socialism" used for decades in class warfare und quite correctly condemned. What I mean under the term "neosocialism" are the ethical and noble characteristics as understood by the uneducated common man from the street.

I wold like my concept of "neosocialism" to be understood as born from the biblical words "Love your neighbour and do good unto those who hate you". And it is a firm principle of mine, that any actions by neosocialists must assure, that no one is interfered with in any way or form, except in the case of visible and convinced criminal conduct. Respect and recognition of human rights must be the ruling principle.

As whith all things, "socialsts" had to learn from bad experiences, but despite setbacks, they steadfastly remained convinced of the superior and noble characteristics of "neosocialism".

Today, the dogmatic "socialism" of class-warfare, as proclaimed by Marx and Engels a century ago and whose political dogma its adherents attempted to impose by force onto their people is obsolete. It is almost unnecessary to mention that the concept of neosocialism is entirely based on the concept of "Democracy" and that they complement one another.

Today we have com sofar, that when someone exposes a deplorable state of affairs and puplicy denounces the bad social conduct of the perpetrators and attempts to put a stop to it, he is branded as a "Socialist" and silenced.

The concept of "democracy" developed over centuries, and slowly grew amongst the people, so likewise in the same way, must the concept of neosocialism grow from within the nations. Morals cannot be imposed through laws. It would be wrong, to impose democratic and neosocialists concept by force to other people. One can only offer assistence, but without deliberate blackmail and only if ones own hous is in order.

It must be pointed out, that achieving the goal of a democratic and neosocialist focused national communitiy, all depends on politicians, having a cosmopolitian and unbigoted upbringing and education, What is important is the early recognition of crafty, powerobsessed individuals and, exercising one's right to vote, preventing those from pursuing theit desires. For vigilance is paramount in order to nip the aberrations in the bud.

CAPITALISM TODAY

The concept of capitalism is the continuation of human development, when it was important for every living creature, to think of himself first, to ensure his own survival. The increase in the number of members of the sippe or tribe (later nations), brought necessarily with it social problems, whose effect were limited, however, since, as mentioned before, the will of the strongest dominated the sippe or tribe. Needless to say, that above mentioned properties were the prerequisite of those ruling people. Capitalistic societies today are characterized by an unending craving for growth, without recognizing, that growth for growth's sake is like a cancer tumor comprised only of the uncontrolled growth of cells. This craving is most often demonstrated in the American media through their continuous advertisements that, firstly, are ridiculously exaggerated and secondly quite obviously insalts the intelligence of the viewers.

It is not my intention to describe the differences between capitalism and neosocialism – that should be general knowledge. I simply wish to point out, based on my knowledge of both and repeate, what I have mentioned already, that a virtualy ideale society is possible, if both adversaries are equally represented and fully respect one another. Capitalism as the engine and neosocialism as the brake. As unlikely as such a development seems in the near future, it is nevertheless important to mobilize the intelligent forces in both camps in order to achieve this goal.

SUPERPOWER DOIMINATES GOVERNMENTS

Furthermore I must especialy mention one thing, and that is today's harmful system of debt, resulting from "Interest" owned, which demeans nations, countries, municipalities and the man on the street. It destroys "Economies" through the monopoly of banks and their control of the money markets. If that monopoly is not broken by the democratic and neosocialst powers (backed by the will of the people), then all efforts to improve the living conditions of the people are in danger of failing.

Several times already, I have brought up the subject of the deplorable state of affairs in the societis of nations with respect to power and financial circumstances. In order to provide a better understanding, I am going to inseret a article from my book "Common Dividend", which I do not want to withfold from intersted readers.

HERE IT COMES

Text books generally differentiate between three governmental powers: the legislature, the executive and the judicial powers.

The legal and sovereign government of every free country must have the power to pass laws, regulating the relationship between sitizens and existing federations, without having to ask permission from a foreign power. This is the exercise of legislatives power.

Likewise, the government of a sovereign country must have the ability to administer the nation in keeping with the laws and its constitution, without submitting its actions to a foreign government for approval. This is the exercise of executive power.

And finally, the government of a sovereign country must have the right to implement the nations laws, to legally prosecute and convict those who transgress and to impose sentences on any citizen of the country without being bound to petition a foreign power. This is the exercise of judicial power.

THE SUPERPOWER

If these three powers – legeslative, executive and judicial- are the constitutional powers of all sovereign governments, there is one power, not yet named, which surpasses the other three and which is prevalent in governments. That prevailing power, which has not been granted authority through the constitution and hence is as unconcerned as a thief exercising his theft, is the – "Financial Power".

That financial power is not the money in our wallets. It is not the money invested in shares and bonds or in bank accounts. Nor is it financial power what governments call inflation, the continuous increase in prices.

No, those are all small fish compared with the power of the superpower being denounced here. It can make our lives hard, brutal and unsettled.

This financial power becomes especialy irresistible when it is exercised by those who have money, control it and are able to grant credit and determine its distribution. So for those reasons one can say, regulate and hold the life blood of the entire economy in their hands, determining the soul of production so that no one dares to oppose their will.

Those strong words may seem extreme to those who have no knowledge of the role, money and credit play in economic life, on the one hand, and the control of the financial power over credit on the other hand.

By what means is this control exercised, you my ask? It is the decision of the financial power to loan money which it does not have but which it creates as a figur in its books in return for "Interest", the amount and term of which it determines. This was mentioned at the beginning of the report and there is nothing more to say about.

The fundamental flaw in the current financial system is that the banks generate monye as a debt and demant "Interest"for it. The obligation of the debtor, be he an individual, a company, a municipality, a city, a province or the state, to pay back the entire amount i.e. with interest, to the banks after a specific term, is impossible, however, because the interest demanded was not generated by the banks. The financiers know full well that the current financial system is flawed to the core and could lead to crises and revolutions. But that is what they want.

The financiers believe that they alone are capable of properly governing mankind, and to do that, the invented the money/debt system. So it is now high time to change the money/debt system, artificialy implemented by the financiers, namely on the ballot box in the next election. The monopoly of the "financiealpower" must be broken and the democratically elected government must take over the "Financiel power". (A nationl credit office)

Such a change in the financial system of a country through the destruction of the private power of banks and financiers and the implementation of a state - run financial power would not be a great change in the handling of finances. Banks would continous to give their clients money and loans, but would obtain the money interest-free from the national credit office and only a single fee would be charged.

To make quite clear what the two above-mentioned currency systems mean, here again a brief summary of the differences.

The first currency system is that under which the state produces the money, e,g, coins and bank notes of various values and puts it into circulation. I.e. the money from which the interest must be paid by the debtors to the banks.

The second currency system is that, which consist only of figures, not of cash, with the banks and the debtors—individuals, municipalities, provinces, cities, countries and governments etc. – who borrowed money and which is recorded under their accounts, i.e. cashless payment transactions.

A STANDING ARMY FOR THE UNITED NATIONS

WORLD FRANK SALVATO
Managing Editor

There are many disturbing issues to contemplate in the world. From the dangers of aggressive Islamofacism to the pomposity and arrogance of the American elected class (and those vying to be included) the world stands witness to myriad threats and power grabs. But two power grabs open the door for the United Nations to both amass sovereign rights and to fund and assemble a military force under its own banner.

That the United Nation is a corrupt and ineffective institution is an understatement. The list of illegal activities and instances of institutionalized bigotry are so numarable that thy weave a tapestry of embarrassment that would incite any governmental body with integrity to disband. Truth be told, they can't even agree on a definition for "terrorism". As they say, absolute power corrupts, absolutely.

An example of the UN's corrupt leadership can be seen in the Oil-for-Food scandal, one of the larger blemishes on the face of the organization. Alas, it is a blemish that the secular—progressive press failed to expose in detail. You see, a few corrupt world leaders – we'll cite Jacque Chirac as a prime example—were utilizing their seats on the UN Security Council to hold the United States and aligned coalition countries at bay while they violated the resolution put in place by that very organization. Their actions defrauded the Oil-for-Food program of millions if not billions of dollars and enriched Saddam Hussein in the process.

For the press to have investigated this bilking of the wold's taxpayers would have been to frame the UN as a fallible entity, an organization capable of being wrong dead wrong. With the "peace at all cost" contingent running roughshod over the media organizations of the free world, it was unacceptable to diminish the reputation of the UN, especially at a time when the Great Satan, President George W Bush, was keeping his post-9/11 pledge to go after terrorist and those nations that aided and abetted them in their endeavors.

Then we have a plethora of examples of the United Nations ineptitude. From peacekeeping missions to global problem solving, their numbers of victories pale in comparison to the numbers of disasters.

In locations from Congo, Liberia, Sierra Leone and Somalia to Darfur and most notably in the 1994 Rwandan genocide, the United Nations has been a dismal failure in providing security and keeping the peace.

In Rwanda, the UN peacekeeping force commander, Lieutenant General Romeo Dallaire, pleaded with his "superiors" at Turtle Bay – at that time the peacekeeping division of the UN was overseen by non other than Kofi Annan – to allow him the authority to circumvent the impending genocide. His repeated requests would be denied.

Dallaire described Annan – who would become UN Secretary General – as being "overly passive in his response" to the reports of a possible genocide. In his book, Shake Hands with the Devil: The failure of Humanity in Rwanda, Gen. Dallaire explicitly states that Annan not only held back UN troops from intervening and from providing more tangible support, but that he failed to provide any response to Dallaire's repeated communiques begging for access to a weapons depositary with precious arms and amunition, something that could have helped save tens if not hundred of thousands of Tutsi lives.

In hindsight, US President Bill Clinton shared his "regret" in his lack of action saying he believed if he had sent just 5,000 military personel to the troubled area more than 500,000 lives could have been saved.

Today in Darfur, we are seeing a reconstitution of the same inane policies and lack of definitive action as in Rwanda circa 1994. As opportunistic Islamofascist elements capitalize on the disorganization of the Sudanese government in an attempt to establish an enclave beholden to Sharia Law, the manipulate the lethargic diplomatic process employed by the UN and all subordinate organizations. The result, ones again, is genocide.

And while many of those who support the charitable efforts of the UN tout their humanitarian missions, i.e. their efforts to feed the starving and treat the diseased, the fact is that most often the food amd medicine provided by the UN literally servs to empower the opressive elements of those affected regions. Food and medicine routinely sit idle at the drop-off locations only to be used by warlords and militas as leverage against the very people the supplies were meant to benefit.

Today, with all these many failures to show for its tenure, the United Nations is now attempting to expand its potentcy in an efford to greate authority beyond its chartered missisions statement:

> "The stated aims of the United Nations are to maintain international peace and security, to safe-guard human rights, to provide a mechanism for international law, and to promote social and economic progress, improve living standarts, and fight diseases."

Nowhere in the UN charter does it give the international body the authority to impose any kind of tax on its member nations or the citizens thereof. Additionally, its charter does not give the body the authority to redefine – especially in a time of peace – the sovereign borders of any nation, regardless of the economic benefit. Yet two initiatives championed by the United Nations establish these authorities.

The law of the Sea Treaty, which President Ronald Reagan brilliantly shunned for the fact that it ceded US sovereignity to the United Nations, allows for the encroachment of UN authority over sovereign US soil and associated waterways. The US Senate is keen to ratify this treaty and President Bush has indicated that he will sign it. Proponents suggest that the treaty solidifies safe passage for our naval vessels throughout the world. Statements this obtuse are seldom heard. That the United States

Navy is the best trained, best eqipped and most potent military force in all oceans of the world is guarantee of safe passage enough. We should n't be giving away offshore minerals rights to satisfy an addiction to unnecessary diplomatic endeavors.

But the most disturbing and the most dangerous initiatives presented of late are the initiatives surrounding the junk science of manmade global warming.

Many will be moved to kneejerk reaction by that thatement. That they are so moved serves as testimony to their status as spineless, misinformed, uneducated followers; not a leader among them.

To declare that the scientifc debat on mans role in the warming and cooling sycle is over, a consensus reached, is to promote a blatant lie. The only consensus that exists is entered into by those politicians and scientists who believe man is a major element in the current global warming cycle. Those who agree that man is a significient cause of global warming have formed a consensus.

Responsible scientist, devoid of political pressure and ecoagenda, have been feverishly attempting to bring forth information that debunks mans influence on the naturally reaccuring global worming and cooling cycles. They have been thwarted every step of the Green movement, environmentallists and that entrepreneuriel opportunist, Al Gore, they have been rendered voiceless by the counter-culture ecogeneration of the 1960s, now in control of mainstream media and the United Nations hierarchy itself.

A shadow of doubt is cast over the legitimacy of the science presented by the UN and its manmade global warming proponents by basic scientific dogma. A scientist is thought to systematical "rule out" detractor arguments and possibilities in ther quest for a theory's validation. In essence, a consensus should never be reached unless it is a consensus that a group of scientists cannot disprove a theory. In the case of manmade global warming there is a sizable contingent of scientists who can disprove manmade global warming but they are being silenced by the ecocommunity, even to the extent of being banned from the most recent climate conference in Bali.

I had mentioned that the manmade global warming hoax was a dangerous one. When we examine the economic impact any global limitation on industry and energy might have, we can certainly see that the world' economic system would be manipulated. That in itself is good enough reasen to look at all aspects of the issue before calculating any actions.

The bigger issue here is less about the imposition of economic limitations on first-worlds, inequitably and more about the establishment of the United Nations as a taxing body.

A panel of UN participants at the United Nations climate conference in Bali – the same conference that the aforementioned scientists were banned from – urgend the UN to create a global tax on carbon dioxide emissions, to help save the Earth from catastrophic man-made global warming. The panel said, the adoption of a tax woulde represent "a global burden sharing system, fair with solidarity and legally binding to all nations."

Let me state this as clearly as possible, the United Nations, an assembly of representatives from sovereign nations, should never be given the ability to impose taxes on any nation or group of people, ever, period.

Once the precedent of the United Nations as a taxing body is established, it opens the door for independently funded entities and missions, entities and missions that could be employed whitout the consent of the majority of member nations and, quite possibly, without the consent of the Security Counsel.

Should the United Nations be given the power to tax the people of the world, to amass an independent financial stream, what is to keep them from raising a military force? The possibility is not far fetched.

Consider that many in the international body would push for self-sufficient peacekeeping forces so that nations` militaries would not be depleted for peacekeeping missions. Once that genie is out of the bottle, the question of its utilization and the catalyst for deployment all become subjective.

Don't get me wrong, I believe that we should be as kind to our planet as possible. I believe we should be moving away from an oil-based energy system as fast as possible, if not for environmental reasons then for the fact that petro- dollars are used by islamofascist nations to fund Wahhabist ideology and terrorist organizations. To that extent the envirofundamentalists and neocons actually have a common ground to work from. But to allow a corrupt and inept international body the authority to raise an independent financial stream when in all actuality the institution's performance warrants cessation.

It was a travesty when Al Gore won the Nobel. It would be an unrecoverable disaster should the UN be allowed to be a taxing body.

The end

MASSIVE CREDIT CRANCH STRIKING NOW

BY MARTIN WEISS

A massive credit crunh is striking, and you sit at a critical juncture like non other in history.

Never before have you seen so much wealth at stake. Never before have you seen such massive threats to that wealth. And, fortunately, never before have investors had such powerful tools to protect themselves from these threats.

In just the last few days, the US Federal Reserve has desperately tried to rescue the nation's $ 10 trillion mortgage market, flooding the banking system with cold cash.

Slashing its discount rate by a half point, and, in a special meeting just this Friday, literally begging America's banks to borrow!

But for the massive US mortgage market-crumbling in 20,000 cities and towns all across America – it's too little too late.

And for the US dollar – already sinking for years und the weight of the largest trade deficits of all times – the sudden flood of more paper dollars is too much, too soon.

That's why I called an emergency teleconference last week and why it was sought out by 15,000 investors from all over the world.

That's also why, this morning, I'm giving you the transcript of the entire hard-hitting, fast-paced event, making this the biggest- and probably most important-Money and Markets issue we've ever published.

This conference-taking place right in the midst of America's worst credit crunch in decades could not be mor timely. And the team we have assembled for you today, led by Dr. Martin Weiss, could not be better suited to help you through it.

Martin Weiss founded his company, Weiss Research, 36 years ago with one paramount goal: To provide for the financial safety and well being of his customers.

Dr.Weiss was recognizced by the US Congress for intodrucing the first evere independent safety ratings in the United States. And he was de-scribed by The New York Times as the first to see the finncial dangers and say so with precision.

So it should not come as no surprise that Dr. Weiss and his team were also among the first to warn you about unusual crisis that America faces right now, today: The breakdown in America's vast market for home mortgages ... and now... a credit crunch that's striking many financial markets.

From the beginning Dr Weiss and his team were way ahead of this cri-sis: Right now, for example, I'm looking at an issue of the Safe Money Report that Dr. Weiss and Mike Larson wrote back in Februar of 2005. Listen to this headline: "REAL ESTATE BOOM AND BUST, three alarming warnings of coming declines"

Or consider this headline from the Safe Money Report of this past February:"MORTGAGE MELTDOWN!" and let me read to you what it says right here and the first page: "Delinquencies and defaults will migrate up the food chain – to larger, more diversified mortgage lenders, even major investment banks". Folks, what I just read to you is todays news! But Martin Weiss and Mike Larson wrote you about it six months ago.

I've been personally following Dr Weiss and his team for a long time now. I've interviewed them on my internatinal radio show over and over again. And I'm continually blown away by their foresight.

But what impresses me even more is that they go far beyond just warnings. They also offer solutions – solutions that not only protect your wealth, but also build your wealth... that not only safeguard you against the dangers, but also help transform those dangers into major profit opportunites.

Martin, the stuffing is hitting the fan right now. Please giv us in a word, your overview of what you see.

Martin Weiss: Complacency!

Tom: I kmow exactly what you're talking about, Martin. I talk to investors all the time. Nearly everyone is saying: "don't worry about it. Stick it out. This will be blow over soon."

Martin: The emperor has no clothes! The little boy has already shouted to the investors in the crowd to announce that the emperor has no clothes. Anyone reading today's headlines can see that the emperor has no clothes. But still, most investors are frozen like a deer in the headlight. They have not yet taken action to protect their assets!

Tom: What's holding them back? Where do you see the greates danger right now? And where do you see the greatest opportunities?

Martin: The gravest danger is in a vast market that few people are paying attention to, and fewer still really undserstand: The US dollar! The US dollar is in grave danger! And some of the greatest opportunities are going to be in the currencies that rise as the dollar falls.

This isn't like the crisis of one decade ago, which started in Thailand and smashed the currencies of Asia. This isn't like the crisis of two decades ago that started in Mexico and then smashed the currancies of Latin America. The epicenter of this earthquake is right her in the United States, and it's going to smash the US dollar.

Tom: OK. But you didn't answer my first question: Why are people still-complacent? What is holding investers from heading to the exits?

Martin: It's all in one three-letter word: F—E—D. The Federal Reserve! It's the deeply held, widely accepted faith that the US Federal Reserve will somehow rescue everyone. They believe the Fed will wave its magic wand and resolve the crisis with money, endless amounts of cold cash. They hope the Fed will absorb all the bad mortgages and all the bad debts.

"Sacrificing the US dollar on the altar of the housing market!"

Tom: Do you agree with that beliefe?

Martin: Ultimately, no. But in short term, the Fed will do everything to try.

Tom: We already know that, don't we. It's has already started, hasn't it?

Martin: Yes. The Fed pumped in $ 24 billion on August 9th. On August 10th, it pumped in another $ 38 billion! And since then, still more!

Tom: So what does that mean?

Martin: It means that, in their zeal to put out the fires here in the United States, they're actually sacrificing the one market that really matters the most in the long term- The US dollar. They're sacrificing the dollar on the altar of the housing market!

Tom: Please connect the dots for all those who have logged on this conference today.

Martin: Anyone who's been paying attention knows that the decline in the US dollar has been a fact of life for years. But so far, that decline has been gradual, and therefore, invisable to most investors.

Now, the Fed is pumping out huge amounts of paper dollars. And that glut of newly printed US dollars inevitably cheapens the value of every dollar – every dollar in your pocket, every dollar in your bank account. Plus, the Fed has pledged to continue pouring as many dollars as needed, for as long as needed. That means the slow, steady erosion in the purchasing power of your dollars, that we've seen for so long, is going to accelerate, and do so wildly.

Tom: In your view, for how long will the Fed try to solve this crisis by throwing paper dollars at it?

Martin: Look what's happening all over America! This is not a local brushfire. We're not talking about a little market. We're talking about the market for US mortgages. The market for mortgages is the larges market for credit in the world. It's larger than the market for US government securit. It's far larger than the commercial and industrial loans to all of America's corporations.

Tom: And we're not just talking about a passing crisis, here today, gone mannana, are we?

Martin: No. It's the worst meltdown in the mortgage market in our lifetime.

Tom: So how long do you think the Fed will keeping pumping out cheaper and cheaper dollars?

Martin: Until the dollar falls so far they can't ignore it any longer... untill they realize the dollar decline is the graeter of the evils... until they finally give up trying to save the housing and mortgage markets.

Tom: Which brings me to my first big question for your team of analysts today: Is the mortgage crisis nearing a climax? Or has it just barly begun?

Martin: I think the person best qualified to answer that question is Mike Larson.

Tom: I've had the pleasure to talking to Mike many times on my show. Mike is you research analyst behind those uncannily accurate housing market forecasts that I talked about a moment ago. He's been Weiss Research's real estate specialist for five years. And more recently, he's become the go-to guy for virtually every financial news reporter in the country, including yours truly.

Mike, I'm an avid reader of your articles in Money and Markets every Friday. And I'm seeing you more and more often on CNBC, Bloomberg and CNN…. in Barron's, the New York Times, the Wall Street Journal. And just recently, you submitted a wheit paper to the Fed and FDIC about this crisis. You held a press conference with some of the nation's leading news organizations. Can you tell us what you told them?

> "What's the next bubble that's going
> to save us from the housing bust?"

Mike Larson: Absolutely! Plus, I'll also tell you what I didn't tell them – namely the events of just the last few days.

First, look at what Fed Chairman Alan Greenspan did a few years ago when the tech market was melting down and the Nasdaq was falling apart.

He slashed interest rates to the bone and helped create a new bubble to bail us out of the tech wreck.

So if the housing bubble is what saved us from the Nasdaq bust, the question now becomes; What's the next bubble that's going to save us from the housing bust.

You've got 14% of subprime mortgages delinquent in the first quarter. You've got surging late payments in the so-called Alt-A mortgages, which are supposed to be somewhat better quality. You've got lenders like Countrywide Financial warning that even their prime credit quality borrowers are having trouble paying back their home equity loans.

It makes perfect sense. It's exactly how you'd expect it to play out. But fore some reason it seams to be a "big surprise" on Wall Street. And some of these numbers are really staggering:

Foreclosure filings in the US were up 87% compared to a year ago this June. We're seeing the percent of nationwide mortgages entering foreclosure at the highest level ever. And we're not even in recession! That's really scary.

What's also scary is that almost every day there's another mortgage lender that's added to the casuality list. There are more than 110 that have either thrown in the towel and gotten out of the mortgage market entirely or that have gone broke.

Home Banc out of Atlanta – broke August 10th. Aegis Mortgage out of Houston – broke August 13th. Martine: That's just a few days ago!

Mike : These companies made $17 billion in mortgages in 2006. So the are not just any tiny companies. And you have probably heard of American Home Mortgage of Long Island. Broke August 6! Last year. they made almost $60 billion in mortgages!

Tom: $60 billion? Unbelievable. but let's talk about the mortgage REITs.

Mike: OK. The point is, you don't have just the lenders that make the loans getting into trouble. You've also got these companies called mortgage REITs – or real estate investment trust – who buy the loans and hold them on their books. Now, Wall Street discovers, all of a sudden, that the underlying credit is so terrible on these loans, they're pulling back the money across the board.

It started in the subprime. It migrated up the food chain. Now it's reaching the big banks – the one everyone has heard of. You walk by their signs evereyday: Well Fargo, National City, Wachowia. They'r starting to eliminate the loan programs they offer. And they'r raising standards on others.

This means that, if you're a homebuyer, you're finding it harder and harder to qualify for a mortgage. And if you're someone who's stuck in one of these bad loans and seeking to refinance it, good luck.

> "Major mortgage company stocks are crushed!
> Down 70%, 80%. 90% this year alone!"

Tom: What about mortgage company stocks?

Mike: Crushed! When you look at the overall Dow or S&P, you may not realizeit it. But some of these stocks are down 70%, 80%, 90%. They've lost much of their value this year alone. It's also hitting the Wall Street banks that are funding these companies: The JP Morgans and the Citigroups of the world.

I see two scenarios:

In the best case scenario, we may see something like the 1988 crisis. Tha's when that gun-slinging hedge fund long Term Capital management and all of its rockes scienties lost billion on high-risk bond markets bets. The bets went sour. The New Yorl Fed steped in to organize a beil out. but the overall economy muddled through.

In a worst-case scenario, you will get somsthing like the savings and loan crisis of the late '80s and early '90s. These kind of events plus interest rate surges – combined to caus mor than 1,ooo S&Ls to fail. The government had to step in with a $ 150 billion bailout. The economy slipped into recession.

Martin: Let me sum up: Regardless of the scenarios, this is far too big for the Fed just to paper over with dollars. And yet that's the only tool they seam to have at their disposal. They're just pumping out more and more paper dollars into the financial markets to try and ease the crisis. For the future of the US dollar. this is a terrible situation.

Tom: Before we talk about the dollar, can we first get closure on this real estate mess? I live on the West Coast. If I have investment real estate in my area, or if I have real estate investments in the stock market, what should I do right now to protect myself?

Martin: We recommend three strategies. The first strategy is to reduce your exposure. If you have investment properties. get rid of them. Sell!

Tom: Wait a second, Martin! We're talking real estate. I can't just call my broker and say "Hi, its Tom, sell everything at the market." it takes time to unwind, to unload properties.

Martin: That's why we also have a second strategy:

Tom: Which is...?

Martin: Which is to buy some hedges, some insurance. And fortunately, there are several available today that are ideal for this situation.

I'm talking about an ETF that's designed to go up 20 percent for every 10 percent decline in the Dow Jones US Real Estate index. when the index goes down, this ETF goes up at double the pace. Would you like that symbol?

Tom: Yes!

Martin: It's SRS, that's good for protecting you from your real estate investments. But as Mike explained, this crisis is migrating up the food chain and beginning to effect banks and other financial companies. So here's another one you can use to protect yourself.

This is also an ETF. It's also designed to go up 20 percent for every 10 percent decline. But instead of being tied to the real estate index, it's tied to the Dow Jones US Financial Index. The symbol is SKF.

One word of warning. These investments are double-edged swords. They surge when real estate or the financial stocks are falling, but if those stocks rally, then these ETF can obviously fall.

So we also have a third strategy, which I think is the better solution a solution that helps you profit from the primary consequence of this crisis- the falling dollar – and to do so continualy, over and over again, month after month.

"Investors in Asia are now very concerned that this mortgage crisis is going to drive the dollar down faster than ever before."

Tom: And that's why we've invited two world- renown experts on the dollar. First, let me introduce Larry Edelson. Larry is one of the world's leading gold analysts, along with his bullish forecast for gold, he has been tirelessly and repeatedly warning about the decline in the buck - the decline that is now unfolding

And man, does this gentleman travel! Larry's just back from Asia, and he's on the call right now to give us the Asian perspective on this crisis.

Where did you go in Asia this time , Larry?

Larry Edelson: I was in Thailand, Singapore, the Philippines and Australia. I go to Asia three or four times a year. This trip was a doozie, and I'm just getting over the jet lag.

But it was also a doozie from an other point of view: I've been traveling to Asia for eight years, and investor confidence in the US markets was usually great, even in the post 9 – 11 period.

But now, for the first time, I've started to hear and see thing that I haven't heard or seen before. Not just among market traders and investors. But also on the street…. talking to taxi drivers….having coffee at Starbucks…. just about everywhere.

For the first time, people in Asia are very very worried about what's happening in the United States. The see the dollar plunging virtually nonstop. And now, they're very concerned that this mortgage crisis is going to drive the dollar down faster than ever before. Conversely, of course, that also means that foreign currencies are going to go up more sharply than ever before.

Tom: Does that mean, international investors are going to start shifting from the US to stronger economies in Asia?

Larry: Going to? They've already been doing it! First, as many of you know, the Asian stock markets have been outperforming the US stock market for some time, dramatically outperforming. Asian economies are fundamentally much stronger than ours. Their GDP growth levels are three, four, fife times the US growth levels.

Between India, China and Southeast Asia, 40% of the world's population is coming out of communist regimes or restrictive socialist democracies that are opening up... and all demanding improved lifstyles at the same time. So the demand factor alone is to keep those economies cooking at higher growth rates than the US.

But Asian investors also have big money in the United States, and they're looking to bring it back.

Tom: Put two and two together for us.

Larry: They see the mortgage crisis. It's all over the headlines there. Not just the business pages, but headlines in the main section: "Mortgage meltdown in the US." "Real estate crash in America."

This is a shock to them. Keep in mind, they don't borrow money like we do. They have a high-saving culture. So the whole notion of going deeply in debt to buy anything, is foreign to them. And this mortgage crisis is really scaring the heck out of them. On top of that, they see the Fed pumping more and more cheap dollars.

Foreign investores are acutely aware of currency values. Unlike us here in the United States, they look at the value of their currency and the value of the dollar every day. They check it daily just like we check the weather or the Dow Jones Industrials. When they see the Fed putting the pedal to the metal on the printing press, they conclude, the dollar has no place to go but down.

That means other currencies vis-`a- vis the dollar – be it the euro, the Swiss franc, the yen, the Australian dollar, ore the Canadian dollarare going to go up against the dollar. So foreign investors are going to do everything they can do to protect themseves

They're shifting out of US dollars. They're bringing their money home. And unfortunately, that creates a vicious cycle. The more they sell, the lower the dollar goes and the mor frightened they get.

Bottom line: The US dollar's purchasing power has been- and is more likely to be than ever before-evaporating because of the crisis. I think the decline you've seen in the dollar so far is just Act One. I think Act Two is beginning now, and it could be very dramatic.

Tom: Let's go straight to the 64-million-dollar question: Specifically how do you profit from this monumental shift?

Martin: You go out of dollars, which are losing value, and you get into foreign currencies, which are rising in value. And to tell us how to do this, I've invited our good friend to join us. His name is Jack Crooks.

"The currency market is, without a doubt the largest market in the World and the most liquid"

Tom: I'm glad you did,Martin. And I'm very pleased to see that Jack Crooks is a long- time friend and associate of Weiss Research. I have interviewed Jack many times. I know that Jack has more than 20 years of experience in the foreign currency market.

That's why many of the world's most influential investment news outlets rely on Jack for timely guidance on currency information.And right now, Jack is working with a revolutionary new breakthrough in the worlds currency market.

Jack, welcome. First tell us about the currency market. Then tell us the revolutionary breakthrough.

Jack Crooks: The currency market is, without doubt, the largest market in the world – and the most liquid. $ 3 trillion dollars a day trade in the currency market. That's more than all of the world's stock markets combined.

What I like most – one of the reasons I specialize in this market- is that there's always a bull market in currencies.It gives you the power to make money regardless of what's happening in the stock market, whether it's soaring or plunging in value.

If real estate is booming, there are opportunities in the currency market. If it's busting, there are opportunities. Same with interest rates – whether soaring or falling. Ditto for bonds and commodities. No matter what's happening elsswhere, opportunities abound in the currency market.

Tom: Why is that?

Jack: It's pretty simple. Currencies are different from stocks, bonds of commodities in that you make money buying and selling one currency against another.

Tom: I think I get the picture. It's like a see-saw. When one is going down, the other one has to be going up. So there is always currencies going up. There is always a bull market. So if you knew, for example that the dollar is going to plunge against another currency, you could buy that currency and make a lot of money, right?

Jack: Yes. But let me add somsthing that you may be missing. It's not just because of the see-saw effect. Equally important is the fact that currenccies move independently from bonds and stocks. The are noncorrelated. What that means to the everage investor is that currencies are a great asset class for diversification.

Tom: Boy, this really intriguing to me. But isn't it true that currencies have always been reserved for the mega-rich only.Why is that?

Jack: In the past, it took a huge account to get involved in the currency market. You probably needed a million dollars just to get the dealer to answer the phone. Plus you had huge risk. The way they were set up in the past, you could lose more – a lot more – than you invested.

But not anymore. Now, for the first time ever, the gates to this market are being flung wide open for average investor.You're seeing a new class of vehicles that give investers virtually unlimited profit potential....but strictly limit their risk.

Tom: Explain why that's so important?

Jack: Until now, there have only been a couple of viable vehicles you could use to trade currencies. One is the currency futures market. In that market, you trade against the major speculators and commercial hedgers in the world.

The other market is the cash foreign exchange market- spot Forex. This is a market that's controlled by the major money center banks and the governments. So in both those markets, you're trading against big, powerful players. You can make a lot of money. They're very liquid, very dynamic. But for the everage investor, one of the big downsides – in either future's or cash Forex – is that you are exposed to unlimited risk,

> "A solution to making money in the currency
> market that's nothing short of revolutionary."

Tom: Jack, you and I have been talking about this months. So I happen to know a little bit about it. The profit opportunities in currencies are unbelievable. But the risk is huge. One tiny move, and unless you have plenty of capital, you could be wiped out. But, you've also told me that now you have a solution, and from everything I've seen, your solution is nothing short of revolutionary. So please tell us exactly what that is.

Jack: It's the new World Currency Options now offered by the Philadelphia Exchange.

The Philly Exchange has been around since in 1790 – they're 217 year old. There are about seven thousand listed stocks and indices traded on the Philadelphia Exchange. Every online and offline broker in the country, and in many foreign countries, trades on the Philadelphia Exchange. It's as easy to trade there as in the New York or American Stock Exchange.

And now, for the first time, they are offering foreign currency options on the Philadelphia Exchange that are just like regular stock options.

Tom: What are the adventages of doing that?

Jack: There are three. The first is the tiny minimums to get into this market. You can buy options in any of the major currencies for as little as $ 100.

Tom: You mean I can start investing in several of this with just a few hundert bucks?

Jack: Yes. The second major advantage is limited risk, and that's extremly important, especially for investors who can't watch these markets 15 hours a day like I do. With the purchase of these options, you can never lose more than the small amounts you investet. So you know your risk on every single trade.

Tom: OK. What's the third adventage?

Jack: Huge leverage.

Tom: How huge are we talking?

Jack: As much as 200 to one, depending on the option. If you get the currency right, that type of leverage will multiply your profits over and over again.

Tom: And these World Currency Options are just like ordinary stock options?

Jack: They are. That's the genius of what the Philly has done. They have the same expiration dates as ordinary stock options. They are very easy to price. The trade in standardized contract sizes across all the major currencies. And the offer the same access through virtually any online or offline broker.

Tom: How are you personally working with the Philadelphia exchange on these World Currency Options?

Jack: I'm working with them to educate the public – how the currency market move, how easy these options are to trade.

Tom: So would it be fair to say that you know more about this then anyone else?

Jack: Haha. I'm not sure about that. But outside of the folks at the exchange itself, it's fair to say that only a handful of people really understand these new instruments or the benefits to the average investor to get into the currency market.

Tom: This is very exciting to me. I've always been fascinated by the currency market. I've have just been leery of the risks. But now, this gives us easy access with total control over risk. Let me ask you this: Would it be fair to say that the folks participating in this call are among the first people to hear about this?

Jack: I'd say yes. because it's fairly new and we haven't done much yet on the education front.

Tom: When you say "we," you're refering to yourself and the folks at the Philadelphia Exchange?

Jack: Reight. We haven"t crankewd up the seminar circuit yet. But the options on the six major currencies are now trading. The volume is ramping up very fast. And they're already available on almost all the broker platforms.

Tom: You mean I could go online right now and trade them?

Jack: Absolutely.

> "You could have an option on the
> Aussie dollar on May 29 and watched
> it soar a staggering 2,867% by July24.
> That's turning $2,000 into $59,334."

Tom: Guy's, I have some numbers provided by your researcch department which I find fascinating. So if you don't mind, I'd like to take a few moments to run through them with you and get your comments. Is that OK with you, Martin?

Martin: Sure, go ahead.

Tom: These are examples of how much money you could have made in currency options, and the first is dated june 15.

On June 15th, if you had bought a call option on the euro and then sold it on July 12th , you could have made 333% in just 27 days.

Martin: It's actually a bit less than that. You have to take out the commissions.

Tom: Oh. right. Here's another one. You could have bought another euro option on June 8 and closed your position 35 days later – on July 13. That one would give you a 7oo% gain. so if you started with $2,000, you would be looking at $16,000. Minus commissions.

Larry: This is Larry, Tom. That sounds like a home- run. Is that one of the most aggressive options on your list?

TOM: No, it's not. But if you want to be more aggressive, here's one you'll like: It's also an option on the euro. It could also have been bought on June 15 and sold on july12. But it jumped 1,oo8% in value one thousand and eight percent. That would have taken $2,000 and turned it into $22,166.

Larry: What time frame was that?

Tom: Just 35 days.

Larry: A thousand percent in just over a month?!

Jack: And that is just the euro. They now have World Currency Options on all the major world currencies, which means it opens up that many more opportunities.

Tom: Exactly. Here's an example on the British pound. If you had bought a call option on the British pound on June 25 and sold it on July 18, you could have made 845%. Initial investment $ 2,000. End result: $18,910. In just over three weeks.

Larry: Is this the best example?

Tom: No. I've got several better ones, which I'll get to you in just a moment. But first, let's talk about the Canadian dollar. On May 21, you could have bought a Canadian dollar option that jumped 667% over the next 64 days- turning your $2,000 into a crisp $15,334.

Plus, here's another call option, also on the Canadian buck. It could have turned $ 2,000 into $ 22,219 between April 1 and July 23!

The Australian dollar has also been particularly strong lately. If you had bought one of its options on April 4th and sold it on July 24, you could have bagged a 758% gain in 111 days. That's enough to turn your $2;000 grubstake into $ 17.692.

And again, that's not the most aggressive one that was available. You could also have bought a Aussie dollar option on May 29, and made a gain of 1,400 % in57 days later. That's your $ 2,000 turning into $ 30,000.

Larry: that's a lot more leverage than most options on stocks or indexes.

Tom: Yes, it certainly is. Here's another example: You could have bought still another, even more aggressive option on the Aussie dollar on May 29 and watched it soar a staggering 2,867% by July 24.

Doing the math, that's turning $2,000 int $ 59,334.

Folks, these are very impressive numbers.

Martin: They are. But I want to add that you can also lose money. It's not a one-way street. The big advantage is that, as with the purchase of any securities options, your losses are strictly limited to what you invest. But your profit potential is unlimited.

Tom: That leads me to the next question: Suppose the dollar rallies and the currencies fall for a while. Certainly you favorite foreign currencies are not going to be going up all the time, are they?

Jack: No. Sometimes there are small rallies in the US dollar, sometimes bigger rallies. That's the beauty of World Currency Options. No matter what the dollar's doing- going up or going down- you can make money. If the foreign currencies are weaker against the dollar, you can simply buy put options and we can make money even as the dollar goes up.

> "A monumental explosion in the Japanese yen has
> already been triggered by the US credit crunch."

Tom: One more important question: What do you plan to recommend next? More call options on the currencies we just talked about?

Jack: Actually, no. It's going to be on another currency, one I'm more bullish on than any of those you talked about.

Tom: Don't keep us guessing. What is it?

Jack: The Japanese yen.

Tom: Because of what Larry said- that their economy is so much stronger?

Jack: Yes. The Asian economies are booming and most of the other Asian currencies have rallied tremendously against the US dollar. The Japanese yen has been the exception. It is without a doubt, the most fundamentally undervalued currency in the world.

The reason is, the Japanese government has done almost everything in its power to keep the yen relative to other currencies. But now, the Japanese economy is growing nonstop. It's gaining momentum. It's jobless rate just fell to the lowest level in 9 years. So the Japanese are going to have to rise interest rates. The market's going to force them to do it. And when that happens, you're going to see it provide a real boost to the Japanese yen.

Martin: I have a question for you, Jack. What is going to trigger this huge move in the yen?

Jack: A monumental explosion in the Japanese yen has already been triggered by all the things you and Mike talked about- the credit crunch.

Let me explain how that works: Major hedge funds and investers around the world have borrowed money in Japan at very low interest rates – massive amounts to fund their risky investments. The hedge funds have taken all that cheap Japanese money and invested it into all these mortgeges in the US. and for a while, they looked like heroes to their investors.

But with the credit crunch, they have to reduce their exposure. That means hundreds of billions of dollars going back to Japan – to buy back yen and repay the loans. And that's going to pure rocket fuel for the yen,

> "The amount for borrowing in the Japanese yen
> is tremendously larger than it was in 1998 when
> the yen surged 20% in one month. So the potential
> for a surge today is almost beyond comprehension."

Martin: Is that what happened the last time we had a crisis like this, back in 1998, when Long Term Capital Management cracked up?

Jack: That's exactly what happened back in 1998. We had a very similar situation – also with low Japanese interest rates, also with investors borrowing large amounts of cheap Japanese money. But as risk began flowing across the globe, investors repaid their loans, and the yen just soared.

Tom: How much did it go up?

Jack: It went up over 20 percent in a month, and kept on rising for over a year. Just to give you some perspective on how that is, we know the euro has been in a huge bull market. But it was only moved 15% against the US dollar in two years. So you can see the potential for a move in the yen is massive.

Tom: Earlier, based on the numbers your research department give me, I talked about options on currencies that exploded as much as 2,867%

higher in just a few weeks. and you're saying the explosion in the Japanese yen could be even bigger?

Jack: Yes. And one more thing: Today, the amount of borrowing in the Japanese yen is tremendously larger than it was in 1998 when the yen surged 20% in one month. So the potential for surge today is almost beyond comprehension.

Tom: The other thing I like about this is that the Japanese yen options are like regular stock options. So I can use my regular broker. I don't have to set up any new account. And I can pay standard discount commissions, even cheap online commissions. Is this correct?

Martin: Correct. And that's one of the reasons we called this conference. Because we're launching a brand new service dedicated exclusively to these World Currency Options.

Tom: I've spent a lot of time looking at this project. In fact you and I have been talking about it for several months. Jack. So if you'll permit me, let me step in here and give our participants some of the highlights. If I say something out of turn, just jump in, OK?

Jack: OK.

Tom: The service is Jack Crooks World Currency Options Alert. It's the world's first and only trading service specifically created to help you profit from The Philadelphia Stock Exchange's new world Currency Options.

For starters, you'll get Jack Crook's "World Currency Option Trading Manual." In the manual, Jack shows you his #1 strategy for selecting the currency options that offer you the greatest profit potential with the least amount of risk. He shows exactly how the Philadelphia Exchange's World Currency Options work and he shows you how he identifies the best ones to trade.

Martin: I'm a risk – averse person. So I' am really pleased to see this providing several risk barriers: The first is diversification – you investing in the currencies of entire nations, not just a few stocks. The second is Jacks close monitoring of each position themselves even in the worst-case scenario, your loss is limited to the small amounts you pay for each of them.

And while we're on the subject of risk, I want to remind you of one more thing: One of the greatest risk of all, in my opinion, is being taken by the folks who do nothing to protect themselves from this dollar crisis.

Larry: How much would you say Jack's trading manual is worth?

Martin: Recently, a course of foreign currencies, which doesn't cover these new World Currency Options, sold for $1,977, and thousands of investors bought it. But you get this manual – Jack Crook's World Currency Options Manual – free with your membership in our new service, the World Currency Options Alert.

Tom: And Martin, I understand that, not only can our listeners test drive World Currency Options Alert at a greatly reduced membership rate, they can get 100% of their money back if they're not trilled with the profits they make. Is that true?

Martin: Of course.

Tom: that means I could sign up today....use Wold Currency Options Alert for two full months.....and then, if I'm not blown away by the profits, I can say goodbye and get a full refand of every penny I paid for my membership, right?

Martin: Sure.

Tom: I've always been intrigued by currencies, how dramatic the moves can be, how huge the leverage is. But I have always been hesitant because of the unlimited risk. Now, with these World Currency Options, I can know exactly what the risk limit is, and I know it will never be exceeded. I also know Jack. And I think he's the best when it comes to currencies. I know of no one better,

Tom: Any other comments, gentlemen?

Larry: This is Larry again. I;ve been away from the office for a few weeks, traveling in Asia. So a lot of what was said here today was news to me. And I can't tell you how over joyed I am to hear about these World Currency Options.

I've traded the currency market inside and out, in the futures and in the crash. And I was always amazed that there was no viable way for the average investor to participate without taking huge risk. No one brought together what got to be most liquid, most wildly profitable market with the investor- friendly instruments like these new options.

I think about Geoge Soros who traded the British pound years ago. He made a billion dollars in a single day. I think about the banks that have been making hundreds of billions of dollars in the currency market. and now the currency market is open to average investors? and with limited risk? That's just terrific.

Tom: Thank you, Larry. Thank you, Martin and team. And thank you, our loyale readers and suscribers, for participating in this conference. Just remember, you don't have much time to take action - protect yourself from this crisis and go for amazing profits. So take full advantage of the knowledge you've gained here today.

Good luck and have a great day!

This is the "End" of the Essay and I believe, that the insight about the actions and greedy character of the persons portrayed should be enough, to give every reader the right perspective. Rudolf Rickes

COMMON DIVIDEND!
TO FIND AN EFFECTIVE CURE FOR POVERTY.

BY LOUIS EVEN

**To solve the financial problems of every country.
To eliminate federal, provincial and municipal debts.
To eliminate taxes that cripple people.**

**Wealth is the thing; money is the symbol.
The symbol should reflect the thing.**

Those who control money and credit have become the masters of our lives.

No one dare breathe againc their will.

The bankers are the creaters and destroyers of money. The creation of money is an act of sovereignity that must not be linked to the banks.

New money, coming into the world, belongs to the citizen themselves,to all citizens, and must be handed over to them in the form of a discount on prices and of a social dividend.

There are a lot of good things in our country, but many individuals and families who need these goods, lack the right to have them, the permission to get them.

Is there anything lacking but money? What is lacking is the purchasing power to make the products go from stores to homes?

MONEY AND WEALTH!

This does not mean that money itself is wealth. Money is not an earthly good, capable of satisfying only a temporal need.

Money is not real wealth. Real wealth consists of all the useful things that satisfy human needs.

Bread, meat, fish, cotton,wood, coal, a car on a good road, a doctor visiting the sick, the knowledge of a science— these are real wealth.

But, in our modern world, each individual does not produce all the things. People must buy from one another. Money is the symbol or token that one gets in return for a thing sold; it is the symbol that one must give in return for a thing that one wants from another.

Wealth is the thing; money is the symbol. The symbol should reflect the thing. There are a lot of things for sale in a country, there must be also a great deal of money to dispose of them. The more the people and the goods, the more the money has to be in circulation that is reqired; otherwise everything stops.

It is prcisely this balance that is lacking today. We have at our disposal almost as great a quantity of goods as we could possibly wish for, thanks to applied science, to new discoveries and to the perfection of machinery. We even have a lot of people without accupations, who represent a potential source of goods. Wehave loads of useless, even pernicious occopatins. We have activities of which the sole end is destuction.

Money is created for the purpose of keeping goods moving. Why then does it not find its way into the hands of the people in the same measure as the flow of goods from the production line?

But then where does money begin, the money, that we lack in order to buy the goods that are not lacking?

The first idea that we keep alive in our minds, without realizing it, is that there is one fixed quantity of money, and that it can not be changed; as if it was the sun, or the rain, or the weather. This idea is utterly wrong; if there is money, it is because those who made it did not make more.

Another prevalent belief about the origin of money is that the Governments make it. This is also incorrect. The Governments today do not create money and complains continiously about not having any. The Governments are taking and borrowing it, but they do not creating the money.

Our standard of living, in a country where money is lacking, is not regulated by the volume of goods produced, but by the amount of money at our disposal to buy these goods. So those who control the volume of money, control our standard of living. Therefore, those who control money and credit, have become the masters of our lives and no one dare to breathe against their will.

TWO KINDS OF MONEY.

Money is whatever serves to pay, to buy; whatever is accepted in exchange for goods and services. There are at present two kinds of money in circulation, one we call pocket money, made of metal or paper; and the other we call book money, made of figures in a ledger. Pocket money is the least important; book money is the most important. It is the bank account with which the Businesses operate. Whit bank accounts, one makes payments or purchases without using metal or paper money. One buys with figures.

I have a bank accout say of $ 40,000. I buy a car wort $ 10,000. I make my payment with a cheque. The car dealer endorses the cheque and deposits it at his bank. The banker then makes changes in two accounts; first that of the car dealer, which he increases by $ 10,000, than mine, which he decreases by $ 10,000. The car dealer had $50,000, he now has $ 51.000 written in his bank account. I had $40,000 in mine. My bank account now shows $ 30,000. Paper money did not move in the country; because of this deal.

SAVINGS AND BORROWINGS.

Book money, like the other type of money, has a beginning. Since book money is a bank account, it comes into existence when a bank acount is opened without money decreasing anywhere, neither in an other bank account nor in anyone's pocket.

The amount in a bank account can be increased in two ways; by saving and by borrowing. There are other ways, but they can be classified under borrowing. The savings accout is a transformation of money. I bring along more pocket money to the banker; he increases my account by this amount. I no longer have that pocket money; I have book money at my disposal. I can get back pocket money by decreasing the amount of book money in my account. It is a simple transformation of money. But since we are trying to find out how money comes into existence, the savings account, being a simple transformation of money, is of no interest to us here.

The borrowing (or loan) account is the account lent by the banker to a borrower.

Say I am a businessman and want to set up a new factory. All I need is money. I go to a bank and borrow $ 100,000 under security. The banker makes me sign a promise to pay back the amount with interest. Then he lends me the $ 100,000.

Is he going to hand me the $ 100,000 in paper money? I do not want it. First it is too risky. Furthermore I am a businessman who buys things at different and widely separated places, through the medium of cheques. What I want is a bank account of $ 100.000 which will make it easier for me to carry on business. The banker will credit my account with $ 100,000, just as if I had brought this amount to the bank. But I did not bring it; I came to get it.

It is a savings account, set up by me? No it is a borrowing account made by the banker himself for me.

MONEY CREATERS.

This account of $100,000 was made, not by me, but by the banker. How did he make it? Did the amount of money in the bank decrease, when the banker lend me $100,000? Well, let us ask he banker.

—Mr. Banker, have you any less money in your vault after having lent me $100,000?

—I haven't gone into my vault.

—Have other people's account been reduced?

—They remain exactly as they were.

—Then what was decreased in the bank?

—Nothing was decreased.

—Yet my account has been increased. From where did the money you lent me come?

—It did not come from anywhere.

—Where was it when I came into the bank?

—It didn't exist.

—And now that it is in my account, it exist. So we can say that it was created.

—Certainly.

—Who created it, and how?

—I did, with my pen and a drop of ink when I inscibe $100,000 to your credit, at

—your request.

—Then you create money?

—The bangs create book money, the money of figures. That's the modern money that

—puts into circulation the other type of money by keeping businesses on the move.

MONEY DESTROYERS.

The bankers, and the bankers alone, make this kind of money; script or bank money. But they do not gaive away the money they crerate. They land it for a certain period of time after which it must be returned to them. The bankers must be repaid.

The bankers claim INTEREST on this money they have created. In my case, the banker will probably demand $ 10,000 from me in enterst, at once. He will withhold it from the loan and I will leave the bank with $ 90,000 in may account, having signed a promise to repay $100,000 in one years time.

But within a year, I must, through the profits I make selling my goods for more then they cost me, build my account up to not less then $100,000.

At the end of the year, I will pay back the loan by making a cheque for $100,000 om my account. The banker will then debit my account by $100,000, therefore taking from me this $100,000 I have drawn from the country by selling my goods. He will not put this money into the account of anyone. No one will be able to draw cheques on this $100,000. It is dead money. Borrowing gives birth to money. Repayment brings about its extinction. The bankers bring money into existence when they make a loan. The bankers send money to the grave when the are repaid. The bankers are therefore also destroyers of money.

And the system so operates that the repayment must be greater than the original loan; the death figures must exceed the birth figures; the destruction must exceed the creation. This seems impossible, and collectively, it is impossible. If I succeed, someone els must go bankrupt, because all together, we are not able to repay more money than has been created.

No one creates what is necessary, to make up the interests, because no one els, except the bankers, creates money. Such a system cannot hold out except for a continuous and ever increasing flow of loans. Hence the system of debts and the strengthening of the dominating power of the money masters.

THE NATIONAL DEBT.

The Government does not create money. When the Government can no longer tax nor borrow from individuals, due to scarcity of money, it borrows from the bank. The operation takes place exactly like mine. As a guarantee, it pledges the whole country. The promise to pay back is the debenture. Again, the loan of the money is an account made by a pen and some ink.

And the country's population finds itself collectively indebted for a production that, ccollectively was made by themselfes. As is the case for war production. It is the case also for peacetime production; roads, bridges, waterworks, schools, churches, etc.

THE MONETARY DEFECT.

The situation comes down to this inconceivable thing: All the money into circulation coms only from the banks. Even metal and paper money, createt by the government, comes into circulation only if it has been released by the bank.

Now the banks put money in circulation only by lending out at "Interest." This means that all the money in circulation comes from the bank and must someday be returned to the banks, increrased with "Interest." The banks remain the owners of the money. We are only the borrowers. Since "Interest" money is not created by the banks, there are people who are necessarily incapable of fulfilling their commitment.

A multiplicity of bankruptcies, both for individuals and companies, mortgage upon mortgage, and an ever-increasing of public "Debt", are the natural fruits of such a system.

DECLINE AND DEGRADATION.

This way of making the country's money, by forcing Governments and individuals into debt, establishes a real dictatorship over Government and individuals alike. The sovereign Government has become a signatory of debts to a small group of profiteers. A minister, who represents over 28 million men, women and children signs unrepayable depts. The banker, who represents a clique interested only in profit and power, manufacture the country's money. This is one striking aspect of the degeneration of power, of which Governments have surrendered their noble function, and have become the servants of private interest.

As for individuals, the scarcity of money develops a mentality of wolfs. In front of plenty, only those who have money—the too scarce symbol of goods—have the right to draw on that plenty. Hence the competition, the tyrany of the "boss," domestic strive. A small number preys on all the others. The great mass of people groans, many in the most degrading poverty.

THE SOCIAL CONTROL OF MONEY.

Book money is a good modern invention that should be retained. But instead of it proceeding from a private pen, in the form of a debt, those figures, which serve as money, should com from the pen of a national organism, elected by the people, in the form of money destined to serve the people. The amount of money should be measured according to the demand of consumers for possible and useful goods. It is therefore the producers and consumers as a whole, the whole of society, which, in producing goods in front of needs, should determine the amount of new money that an organism, acting in the name of society, should put in circulation from time to time, in accordance with the country's developments.

Thus the people would recover their right to live full lives, in accordance with the country's resources and the great possibilities of modern production.

WHO OWNS THE NEW MONEY?

Money should therefore be put into circulation according to the rate of production and as the needs of distribution dictate.

But to whom does this new money belong when it comes into circulation in the country?—This money belongs to the citizens themselves. It does not belong to the Government, which is not the owner of the country, but only the protector of the common good; nor does it belong to the accoutants of the national moneytary organism: like judges, the carry out a social function and are paid, according to law, by society for thair services.

To which citizens?—To all. This money is not a salary. It is new money injected into the public, so that the people, as consumers, may obtain goods they need which are already made or easily realizable, which are awaiting only sufficient purchasing power for them to be produced.

There is no other way, in all fairness, of putting this new money into circulation then by distributing it equally among all citizens, without exception. Such a sharing also makes it possible to derive the maximum benefit from the money; since it reaches into every corner of the country.

Let us suppose that the accountents, who act in the name of the nation, find it necessary to issue another $1 billion in order to meet the latest needs of the country. This issuance could take the form of book money, the inscription of figures in ledgers, as the bankers do today. Since there are 28 million Canadians and 1 billio dollars to share, every sitizen will get about $36 in each citizen's account. Such individual account could easily be looked after by the local post offices, or by any branches of a bank owned by the nation.

To each the dividend.

Whenever it might become necessary to increase the amont of money in a country, each man, women and child, regardless of age,would thus get his or her share of the new stage of progress that makes the new money necessary. This is not a payment for a job done but a dividend to each one for his share in a common capital.

The social organization, which makes it possible for our community to produce goods a hundred time mor and better than if we would live in isolation and had to care for our self, is yours as well as mine, and must be worth something to you as it is to me.

Science, which makes industry able to multiply production almost more and more whitout labour, is a heritage passed on to each generation and each member of every generation should have a share in this legacy.

The "Common Dividend", as it is called to understand the system better, will ensure that you get your share, or at least a major portion of it. A better administration, taken away the "Curse of Scarsity" of the money supply—on purpose established for centuries by the "Money Masters"—will see to it, that you get your share.

It is also this "Dividend" that will recognize you as a member of the human species, in virtue of which you are entitled to a share of the world's goods, at least the necessary share to exercise your right to live.

PRICE REGULATIONS.

The dividend added to salaries and other sources of income goes to make up purchasing power. The dividend to all would not do away with wages and salaries of those employed in production. It is obvious, that there would still be the difference in income between a man having only the dividend and a man having the dividend and salary.

But there are people who do not need all their money for their livelihood and prefer saving or investing some of it. This reduces the effective global puchasing power. Only the money used to bay makes up immediate and effective purchasing power.

For this reason and others, the balance between prices and purchasing power is not reached solely by given a dividend to all. However, Common Dividend provides for this balance a regulating mechanism which, while respecting the freedom of each one, makes the savings of the wealthy profitable to all and at the same time prevents any inflation.

This mechanism is the adjusted price (but by no means a fixed price); it is also called the compensated price, or the compensated retail discount.

There is nothing artificial or arbitrary about it. It reflects exactly the facts about production and the consumption of real wealth.

If, for example, the national accounts show that in one year the country's total production has reached a value of say 3o billion dollars, and during the same year, total consumption (depreciation included) has been 24 billion dollares, what can one conclude? One can conclude that, while the country has coused $ 24 billion of wealth to disappear through consumption and depreciation, it has created $30 billion of currency. So the creation of $ 30billion of money has actualy cost collectively anly $24 billion.

The real price is lower then the accounting price. For the population to fully reap the fruit of work, it must be given a discount of $6 billion; that is, pay anly 24 for what is in the books at 30.

Tu this end, the "National Moneytary Organisation" will decree a general discount of 20% on all retail sales for the next period. If I buy an article at $10, I will have to pay only $ 8.

But, in order to stay in business, the retailor and the producer must still recover all of their expenditures. For this reason, the same moneytary system will compensate the retailor, by creating the necessary amount of money. For instance, as in the simple example mentioned before, for the $10 article, I give $ 8 to the retailor. Upon presenting of his sales voucher to the local branch of thr moneytary organism, the retailor will get the $2 which was discounted. This creation of money by this "Nationale Moneytary Organisation" in no way couses inflation since, on the contrary, it is linked to a lowering of all prices for the buyer.

Moreover, appropriated methods would attach this compensation, which favours the retailor as much as the buyer, to agreements fully respecting cost prices, but holding the profit margin in the limits of a percentage agreed upon as beeing adequate in each business sector. The standard of living would be regulated by the amount of goods available, since the amount of money would be regulated by the amount of goods produced. Money becomes what it should be; an instrument to sell products, and not a weapon to confer power to individuals.

For production requiring human labour, money would come through wages and salaries; for easy production, easy money; abundant production. abundant money; automatic production, free money; for production increased by a common capital, through the factor of organized society, issued be a social source and distributed to each and everyone.

RESULT: SECURITY.

The first thing that man looks for, on a temporal viewpoint is "Security," the preservation of his life. It is to ensure himself a better protection against enemies— wild beasts, hunger, cold—that he joins forces with his fellow men. He is even ready to sacrifice a certain degree of his freedom in order to have at least a minimum of economic security. No, what prevents us from feeling secure about tomorrow is our fears of not having enough income, enough money to buy a sufficient share of things. Nothing gives this security today.

If money were to keep in step with production, if it were sufficient distributed as to guarantee by law that each one had enough to ward off want, we should immediately witness the birth of economic security in a country that lacks nothing. Well, it is this security for each and everyone, without exception, that the "CommonDividend" moneytary system would guarantee. From this very security ensues freedom, a freedom to man that, once guaranteed the necessitive of live, he will prefer to keep his freedom, his dignity rather than crawl or fight to get more comfort. No whip of scarcity of money anymore.

RESULT: GOVERNMENT.

If governments today do not actually govern, it is because they have become the servants of private interests. They obligate themselves for debts to bankers who manufactur money. Even the most capable men, when they take the rains of government, are helpless to resist these creaters of debt.

Instead of governing the country according to the coutry's real possibilites, they have to govern by a regime based on principle of the "SCARCITY" of money. The country's pilots stand before a helm handcuffed.

Those forms of government closest to the people, such as municipal governments, find themselves completely buffeld by the problem of trying to find money where there is none. They can bring some into existing, for urgent matters, only by increasing the country's nationale debt and the burden of taxes, without corresponding services.

Common Dividend would restore to the governments their proper functions. Money issuing would be brought back to the government by establishing a proposed "NATIONALE MONEYTARY ORGANISATION," which would be under the control of the people themselve and would put money, the "Life Blood of Economic Life" back in circulation.

Once freed from the unsolvable budgetary nightmares, and independed of the monitary powers in the past, the GOVERNMENTS would be in a better position to intervene when-ever the security of the social order is threatened by saboteurs, terrorists, etc.

A German's View
On Islam.

A man whose family was German aristocracy prior to World War II owned a number of large industries and estates. When asked how many Gerrman people were true Nazis? The answer he gave can guide our attitude toward fanaticism.

Very few people were true Nazis 'he said', but many enjoyed the return of German pride, and meny more were too busy to care. I was one of those who just thought the Nazis, were a bunch of fools. So, the majority just sat back and let it all happen. Then, before we knew it, they owned us, and we had lost control, and the end of the world had come. My family lost everything. I ended up in a concentration camp and the Allies destroyed my factories.

We are told again and again by 'experts' and 'talking heads' that Islam is the religion of peace, and that the vast majority of Muslims just want to live in peace.

Although this unqualified assertion my be true, it is entirely irrelevant. It is meaningless fluff, meant to make us feel better, and meant to somehow diminish the spectre of fanatics rampaging across the globe in the name of Islam. The fact is the fanatics rule Islam at this moment in history.

It is the fanatics who march. It is the fanatics who sytematically slaughter Christian or tribal groups in Africa and are gradually taking over the entire continent in an Islamic wave.

It is fanatics who bomb, behead, murder or honour kill. It is the fanatics who take over mosque after mosque. It is the fanatics who zealously spred the stoning and hanging of rape victims and homosexuals. The hard quantifiable fact is that the 'peaceful majority,' the 'silent majority' is cowed and extraneous.

Communist Russia was comprised of Russions who wanted to live in peace, yet the Russian Communist were responsible for the murder of about 20 million people. The peaceful majority were irrelevant. China's huge population was peaceful as well, but Chinese Communists managed to kill a staggering 70 million people.

The everage Japanese individual prior to World War II was not a war-mongering sadist. Yet, Japan murdered and slaughtered its way across South East Asia in an orgy of killing that included the systematic murder of 12 million Chinese civilians; most killed by sword, shovel, and bayonet. And who can forget Rwanda, which collapsed into butchery. Could it not be said that the majority of Rwandans were 'peace loving'?

History lessons are often incredibly simple and blunt, yet for all our powers of reason we often miss the most basic and uncomplicated points:

> Peace –loving Muslims have been made irrelevant by their silence.

> Peace- loving Muslims will become our enemy if they don't speak up, because like my friend from Germany, thy will awaken one day and find that the fanatics own them, and the end of the world will have begun for them. Peace –loving Germans, Japanese, Chinese, Russians, Serbs, Afghanis, Iraquis, Palestinians, Somalis, Nigerians, Algerians, and many others have died because the peaceful majority did not speak up untill it was to late. As for us who watch it all unfold; we must pay attention to the only group that counts; the "Fanatics" who threaten our way of life.

ENLIGHTENED PERSPECTIVE.

If you will take time to read this, I will promise you'll com away with an enlightened perspective. The subjects covered affect us all on a daily basis!

The're written by Andy Roony, a man who has the gift of saying so much with a few words. Enjoy....

I've learned.... That the best classroom in the world is at the feet of an eldery person.

I've learned....That when you are in love, it shows.

I've learned....That just one person saying to me, 'You have made my day!' makes my day.

I've learned....That having a child fall asleep in your arms is one of the most peaceful feeling in the world.

I've learned....That being kind is more important than being right.

I've learned....That you should never say no to a gift from a child.

I've learned....That I can always pray for someone when I don't have the strenght to help him in some other way.

I've leanred.... That no matter how serious your life requires you to be, everyone needs a friend to act goofy with.

I've learned....That sometimes all a person needs is a hand to hold and a heart to understand.

I've learned....That simple walks with my father around the block on summer nights when I was a child did wonders for me as an adult.

I've learned....That life is like a roll of toilet paper, the closer it gets to the end, the faster it goes.

I've learned....That we should be glad God doesn't give us everything we ask for.

I've learned.... That momey doesn't buy class.

I've learned.... That it's those small daily happenings thay make life so spectacular.

I've learned....That under everyone's hard shell is someone who wants to be appreciated and loved.

I've learned.... That to ignore the facts does not change the facts.

I've learned....That when you plan to get even with someone, you are only letting that person continue to hurt you.

I've learned.... That love, not time, heals all wounds.

I've learned.... That the easiest way for me to grow as a person is to surround myself with people smarter then I am.

I've learned....That everyone you meet deserves to be greated with a smile.

I've learned….That no one is perfect until you fall in love with him.

I've learned…. That life is tough, but I'm tougher.

I've learned….That opportunities are never lost; someone will take the one you miss.

I've learned….That when you harbor bitterness, happiness will dock elsewhere.

I've learned….That I wish I could have told my Mom that I love her on more time before she passed away.

I've learned….That one should keep his words both soft and tender, because tomorrow he may have to eat them.

I've learned….That a smile is an inexpensive way to improve your looks.

I've learned….That when your newly born grandchild holds your little finger in his little fist, that you are hooked for life.

I've learned….That everyone wants to live on top of the mountain, but all the happiness and growth occurs while you're climbing it.

I've learned….That the less time I have to work with, the more things I get done.

To all of you…. Make sure you read all the way down to the last sentense.

Rudolf Rickes!

ANARCHISM AND DOUBLETHINK.

AGAIN: JOE SOBRAN

If you want to survive in this harsh world, the argument runs, you'd better seek the protection of a state, just as, in a tough neighborhood, you may have to join one gang or the other. Anarchism, in this view, is simply not an option. It's only a dream.

To live, then, is to be the slave of a state, a reasonably mild state, an Athens rather than a Sparta, whose rule is bearable but whose survival is viable. Of course it's easy for us to forget that many men are more at home in a Sparta then in an Athens. The taste for freedom, including respect for others freedom, is far from universal, or we would be all free.

This is a powerful argument, and I won't try to refute it here. But at most it proves only that the state is a necessary evil and that the rule of force is inescapable. Even if we are all doomed to live under the state, it doesn't follow that there is, or even can be, such a thing as a good state.

Of course some states are worse than others, and the differences matter. Sometimes their subjects can impose limits on them – bills of rights, for example. But since the state is finally a monopoly of force, such limits are always tenuous and unstable. The state's excuse for being, is its protective function, but no that I no of has ever been confined to this role for long. It soon becomes aggressive, either toward neighbouring communites or, mor often, ageinst its own subjects.

The remarkable fact is that men are so loyal to the states that rule them. They actually idealize and take pride in their rulers. It may be obvious to outsiders that those rulers are tyrants, but their subjects seldom see it that way. They are often ready, and proud, to fight and die for the man who theoretically should protect them! It's like sacrificing your life to save your bodyguard.

Consider that strange creature, the American conservative. He constantly, and rightly, complains that his government is oppressive. At the same time, he insists that his country is the freest on earth. What's more, he is proud that it's also the most militarily powerful on earth. Yet he also thinks his freedom is in constant peril from foreign threats, and only the state can preserve it from immnent destruction.

George Orwell gave us the word "doublethink" for the ability to hold two contradictory views simultaneusly. Conservatives have now achived doublethink and are approaching something like triplethink. They forget that the state is at best a necessary evil, a threat to liberty, and extol their own state as a positive good, even glorious thing we should take pride in. They quote Lord Acton – "All power tends to corrupt" etc – and celebrate American power. Which is it?

Thus does a "necessary evil" become an idol. Maybe we're stuck with it. But do we have to worship it?

The end.

THE GREATEST DECEPTION OF ALL TIMES.
WHEN DO OUR POLITICIANS WAKE UP?

The greatest and far-reaching economic scandal in our days takes place, because of manipulations on the currencies and money systems. The money deception has for the first time a global Dimension becouse it effects all nations of the worlds ecomomies the same, and no government is anymore able to stop or control it, and because of obsolate regulations and laws, formal even legalize occurs.

The firm step away from states money was 1913 after the formation of the "Federal Reserve Bank- (FED)- in the USA. Already by the end of the 19th century, starting the banks, which where controld by the "Rothschild Imperium" a greate campaign, to seize control of the Rich US Economy. The european Rotshilds financed the J.P. Morgan & Co. Bank, the Bank Kuhn Loeb &Co.,John D. Rockefellers Standard Oil Co., Edward Harrimans Railway and Andrew Carnegies Steelworks.

Already about 1900, dispatched the Rotschilds Paul Warburg, one of their agents, in the USA, in order to work together with the Kuhn & Lob bank. Jacob Schiff and Paul Warburg launched a campaign to create the "Federal Reserve Bank" (FED) as a secure installed privat Central

Bank in America. Under the guidance of both "Great Finance Groups, Rotschild and Rockefeller" the obtained the right with their (FED) to issue their own money which was also legal tender, and fore which at first, the American Govern-ment still guaranteerte. The introduction of the (FED) in 1913 made it possible now, fore the internationale Bankiers to solidify their financial power in the USA. Paul Warburg became the first chairman of the (FED).

The decision to establish the(FED) was followed by the 16th addition of the American Constitution, which allowed the government, to tax the personal properety of the citizen. This was the consequence of it, that the US Goverement now could not anymore print its own money. Whit this had the internationale Bankingsystem with a bold stroke a grip on the private wealth of the citizens of the United States obtained.

From this point of time on, were the important chare holders of the (FED) :

1. **The Rotschildbanks in Paris and London,**

2. **Lazard Brothers Bank in Paris,**

3. **Israel Moses Seif Bank in Italy,**

4. **Warburg Bank in Amsterdam and Hamburg,**

5. **Lehmann Bank in New York,**

6. **Kuhn Loeb & Co. Bank in New York,**

7. **Rockefellers Chase Manhatten Bank in New York,**

8. **Goldman Sachs Bank in New York.**

After the First World War, all Goldreservs in the world were bought up by the private Bank(FED) with the result, that many other currencies could not keep their Gold Standard and ended up in a Deflation – the first Crisis of the world Economy. Also during the time of the same World War, the Americans insisted upon payment in Gold for the delivery of Armament to the belligerent nations. Germanies Gold, considered as War Booty after the War, was confiscatet from the victorious nations. So they aquired more then 30,000 Tons of Gold from the World alone in the USA. This Gold did serve as security for the US Dollar. Since however a greater part of Dollars were deposited in the Centralbanks of the world as a reserve currency, could the USA print more Dollars and issue them as there was a Gold Basis available. The country's of the world needed Dollars because to buy row materials, they needed Dollars in which the were only traded. Beside the Gold, the US-Dollar became also stronger in the other Central Banks and the main choice for currency reserves. The rule of the Dollar over the world had began.

In 1971, US - President Richard Nixon (1969 – 1974, 37th President of the USA) cancelled the treaty of redeeming the obligation's of Dollars in Gold (the Gold Dollar standard) and at the same time, cancelled the liability of the state. Since that time, are Dollarnot's neither real through Gold ore through States liability secured, also a free private currency of the Federal Reserve Bank (FED). And those from the (FED) itself determined amountes of Dollar – Circulations (the FED did publish since March 2006 the Money Circulaton of the US Dollar "M" not any more) bacame an unsolvable problem. Because during the last 30 years, the amount of Products and other wares grow 4 times, but the amount of Money grew 40 times.

But how functions this Private Bank which has the right to print those Dollars? The (FED) produces "Federal Reserve Banknotes = Paper-dollars which will be lend and become Obligations to the US Govern-ment, and serve the (FED) as security. These Obligations will be held by the Banks which again draws "Interst" from them fore every year. Clever not? Already 1992 was the value of the Obligatios, with which the Privat Banks of the (FED) held onto almost 5 Billiarden US Dollars plus the INTEREST payments and the Debt of the of the American Cit-izen grow constantly. This whole unbelievable fortune has been created by the (FED) because, as mentionet before, in lending Money to the US – Government and demand high Interest for it. As equivalent fore it, they became colorfully printed paper, called "Dollar."

Over again, the US Dollar is not created by the US-Government, but by the (FED), an amalgamation of private banks, which dispositions the money to the US Government and in return demands high Interest. This Swindle was berely noticed as such to begin with. To be addeed comes, that the (FED) through those Obligations of the US – Goverment, the Hypothecary Law, state and privat, became therewith the Landowner of the whole United States of America. Countless Legal Proceedings, to revoke the (FED) Law, remained uncuccessful. The first one who attemoted it, was then President John F. Kennedy, who on the 4th of June 1963 a Presidentialles Document produste (execotive order number 11110.) in order to dethrone the (FED). Shortly later, he was assassinated, probably by his own security gard. His successor, Lyndon B. Johnsons first order was to revoke exactly these official order from John F. Kennedy on his return flight from Dallas.

And today? With all means to there disposal, attempting the Private Banks their enorme incumbency of US Dollars through their Deception to maintain and secure them. States, which want there internationale trade relations to convert to Euro basics, will be as "Terroristen" declared (Irak, Iran, Venezuela) and will be forced, goods for worthless Dollars to the US to supply, and because of the unrestrained increase in the currency of the High Finanze, she has unlimited liqued resources of worthless Dollars, enables it to shop worldweit. Worldweit are also the central banks forced, the worthless Dollars as currencies – reserves to keep. The US Dollar is the private Money of the High Finanze, from no-one but themselves guaranteed, for Profitmaximierung misused, unchecked enlarged and as instrument of their desire of World-mastery and remedy for robbery of row materials of the world, misused.

The End: Rudolf Rickes.

THE TROUBLE WITH DEMOCRACY!

It is the best of all bad Government Systems but for many not anymore good enough – The Democracy leaves some people cold. Many see them from Turbocapitalism undermined, from Special Interest eroded. The Export of the Democracy Model in the way of the USA, is Worldwide wrecked – many Afrikans and Asiens believe on Autokratic Models. What should we do? Erich Follath.

The future of the Democracy. When the Wall happened to fall in Berlin, two decades ago, it looked as had the Democracy won a victory for the eternity. "The sentence Freedom fore everyone" became from a demand a concrete **Hope**. But this did not come true. Country's like China or Russia took over the capitalism from the West, but not the understanding of Democracy and Human Rights. Contrary to this, the Democracy became a new Competitor namely the Authoritarian State which is economically very successful, and became Models for African and Asien Nations.

The question for the West is in coming years, not so much, which State with a friendly attitude towards the western Parliamentary Model, becomes a companion and employ's it for themselves? That means, that the USA and other Democraties must break the attraction of authoritarian Powers. There is no doubt, that some things are going easier in a tight guided state. Who would not prefer, to make Deals in a country without free Tradeuniens? Obvious, the Democracy makes humans not automatic happy, but happy humans , will create a Democracy. "Good Governance" fore the well being of the People is not possibly without participation of the people. A lasting Democracy requires more than an Election Campain. It need's a functional civil society with basically confidence in its institutionen, with a readiness fore a compromise and respect for the law. Simple said: Without the rule of the law and its competence, not in there own pockets working Politicians.

After almost two decades of prevailing hopefully developments suffers the Democracy a painful rebound. The Experts register a worldweit decline of the Democracy as a Model form of state. There are regions, which are cultural not ready to this way of life in a Democracy, which fore us appears so attractive. What the Democracy im westlichen Sense from the begin on so excellent made, was the promise of justice and joint denomination in the Governments. If this dream will ever materialice in the majority of state's in the world, time will tell. The future does not look very promising.

The End: Rudolf Rickes

THE BANK OF POLAND IS PUT AT THE SERVICE OF THE PEOPLE.

The leaders of three parties have often said, that the Bank of Poland should be used to finance the nation with interest free loans, and that it was stupid for a government to borrow at interest money, that it can create itself without it.

The international Finaciers would like every government to give up their sovereign right to use their central banks (and even have it written in their constitutions as it is the case with the European Union), for they know very well that if only one country takes back the control of the issue of its own currency, that would be a deadly blow to their monopoly of the creation of Money, since this country would show the entire world the proof, that a country can be run without borrowing from private banks, and the other countries would soon follow this example.

If this money is issued for new production, and paid back (only the principal, since there is no Interest) as the new production is consumed, there is no risk of inflation, and Poland will experience an era of prosperity never seen before. With an honest money system, it will be possible to finance, debt free, all that is physically feasible, to answer the needs of the population. The financial circles have every reason to be worried, for the Common Divident solution will follow as the next change. If the solution becomes well known among the population, the Polish Government will hav the support to apply this just reform, despite all the opposition of the internationale Bankers. Let Poland set the example to the whole world.

The End: Rudolf Rickes

In defence Of The Booklet The New United Nations In Year 2050,

While I was writing my last Booklet "NUN in 2050", which I considered as the culmination of my writing, the feeling entered my mind, that a reader would not see my intention with clarity although I mentioned before, that as a subject, it is only futuristic and time-less in substance. They will consider it as an Utopy and therefore condemn the Booklet and the Author as a naive and insane Phantast, although my effort was only to show a glimmer of hope and a possible way to achieve that in peace.

This futuristig essay describes what might happen, when the present "Money Debt Slavery System" era has not the trust anymore of the whole population of all Nations, which voted and elected people in power which were animated with the spirit of "Social Jusatice" and "Common Divident" as a better replacement. As a prerequisite to make this aim com true, it is unquestionable, that the populations are educated wholly and solely with the fore-mentioned spirit. Whoever doubts, that the time is not right for such an extrem change, I would like to remind him, that during the history of mankind about several thousands of years, ther were always changes happening in decades which we call now "Developments", up to the day right now. So it will be also with that what we discusse here. I don't like to explain in detail, what is just said here now, it would create a whole book by itself and I trust the scientific knowledge of the reader.

As a prominent example, the exploitation and mistreatment of humans as slaves was condoned by all nations and societis for thousands of years. Today, this has finally been proclaimed immoral and considered illegal by 98% of the world.

Throughout history, individuals have stood up out of personal honour and sympathy for the slaves despite the hoplessness of their cause to fight for the abolishment of slavery just as I am fighting to overcome the evils of economic and money debt slavery by the controlling elite.

Improving the wrongs to a degree, is already a success,

The Author: Rudolf Rickes.

ON TERRORISM

Barely a day passes without an article about terrorists being published in the news media, rightfully condemning their attacks. According to the commentators, terrorists are criminals; an evil that cannot be eradicated. However, the cause of terrorism is a simple one and easily explained using the following simile:

If a carpenter gets a splinter in his hand and he fails to remove it right away, his body will respond to the intruder and cause the wound to fester. Terrorism is just like that: If a country in arrogant moralistic zeal, attempts to force its values, such as democracy, onto another country by violent means, the effected country will resist the intruder and mobilize its defenses. The intruder will declare this reaction to be "terrorismus" and fight it.

As we know, the American world power regards itself as the champion of our Western civilization in charge of spreading democracy worldwide. This leads to conflict with th traditions of Islam, whose followers will, as described, fight the intruder with the means available to them:

And thus, terrorism is born.

As we have seen, these so called terrorists have a plausible and legitimate reason to fight the intruder. That their cause also attracts criminals, who spot a perfect opportunity to act with their base impulses, is in the nature of things but not the defining characteristic.

FROM SOCIALISM TO NEO-SOCIALISM.

In the beginning and for centuries, the socialist idea could be summed up as Winston Churchill once did it so succinctly: "Take from the rich and give it to the poor". Over the course of time, legions of allegedly socialist politicians focused on regarding the rich as the enemy of the poor, without even understanding the deeper meanings of socialism, without even understanding that poverty can be of one's own making— and this is what gave the concept of "socialist" its bad name. The term was used despairingly by hostile propaganda, tarnishing its otherwise notable character.

"Neo-socialism", as I could like it to be seen, has its foundation in the biblical enjoinder to love one's neighbor and to render blessing for evil. I have also coined the term "Neo Social Justice" which is close to the "Universal Declaration of Human Rights", proclaimed with lots of fanfare and even more propaganda by Mrs. Eleanor Roosevelt, widow of the former U.S. president Franklin Roosevelt, the effects of which came close to those of a revolution.

WHAT ARE THE ORIGINS OF OUR ADVANCED CIVILIZATION?

Many may ask themselves this question without pursuing it further. Our civilization did not simply come into being on its own accord; it is the result of a struggle between influences that have affected and shaped it over the millennia.

Firstly, there is the Christian religion that supplied the foundation. It's to put it simply—internal organizational structure, very close to that of the feudal form of governance, naturally infused with religious aspect and characteristics. Skeptics and apostates were punished as sinners.

Then, like a bright spot on the spiritual horizon, the aforementioned democracy made it's appearance, given new impulses to intellectual life. Then there was the politically current of "liberalism" that became decisive for the freedom of thought and made short of religions' narrow-mindedness. Not to be overlooked, when speaking of this period, there were the social deprivations which led to awakening of socialist ideas. There were the workers who, to protect themselves from exploitation, came up with the concept of "unions". And, to complete the mosaic, there were all sorts of parties striving for power and contributing their part to the formation of our society.